back home

back home

JULIA KELLER

SCHOLASTIC INC.
New York Toronto London Auckland
Sydney Mexico City New Delhi Hong Kong

ISBN 978-0-545-26010-7

Published by Scholastic Inc., 557 Broadway, New York, NY 10012, by arrangement with Egmont USA. SCHOLASTIC and associated logos are trademarks and/or registered trademarks of Scholastic Inc.

12 11 10 9 8 7 6 5 4 3 2 1   10 11 12 13 14 15/0

Printed in the U.S.A.   40

First Scholastic printing, March 2010

Dedicated to our military veterans
and their families.

❚ ❚ ❚ ❚ ❚ ❚ ❚

Memory turns the truth into a story.

———

SAM TAYLOR

1. FORT

Everybody needs a fort.

You can live without a lot of things in your life, things other people might say you need. But all you really need is a fort. It can be small, but it has to be sturdy. It's the place you can go when you don't have anywhere else to go. A place where there won't be a lot of questions. A place where people won't be looking at you or making judgments or assumptions about you. A fort is all about protection.

When you get older, you learn how to make other kinds of forts. You don't have to count on the one in your backyard anymore. You have your friends and your plans and your books. You have all the things you now know about the world: those things keep you safe. But for a while, you need an actual fort, like the one we built behind the house that summer.

A fort with a sheet of plywood for the roof, and a dirt floor. A decent, simple fort. When you go inside it, the whole thing feels like it's sort of squishing in around you, but in a good way. It feels like it feels when you're waiting for the school bus on a cold day, and your friends are on all sides of you, and everybody's wearing heavy coats.

I had that kind of fort. Every time I hung out there, my fort would get a little bit smaller. At least that's how I remember it, anyway. And I liked that. I liked the idea that I could touch the walls without leaning over or stretching, that when I sat there, everything was close and tight. The whole world was there at my fingertips. The whole world was exactly where I needed it to be.

Maybe I liked it because right after that, everything changed.

I was thirteen that summer.

The summer before my father came back home.

There was a time when I thought my father could do anything. Then I didn't think that anymore.

You believe certain things about your parents. They run the world. They run *your* world, and that's the only world that really matters. You carry that idea around with you, everywhere you go. But someday that has to change, because you change.

Your parents don't change.

Except that sometimes they do. And that ended up being one of the worst parts of everything that was about to happen. Because parents aren't supposed to change. Change is for when you're a lot younger, when you're still on your way somewhere. Parents have had their shot at growing up and changing and becoming something different, if that's what they decide to do.

Change is great. It's what keeps life from getting boring. But it should really happen before you officially become an adult. That's how it's supposed to work.

My father, Edward Jerome Browning Jr., changed so much that it just threw off all of my ideas about parents and change. It wrecked my whole theory.

I had everything pretty well figured out. I had it down.

And then he came back.

My mother likes to make speeches. She's one of those people who believes she can get out ahead of things—bad things, I mean—by preparing everybody in advance, by speaking slowly and carefully about the sadness or confusion or frustration you're about to feel. It's almost like she's trying to put a frame around things, to sort of steer the world in the right direction, or at least have a say in how other people feel. I don't mind. I know why she does that. Adults need to have a lot of control over what happens. And sometimes they don't. Sometimes nobody does.

You can tell she works on her speeches. She might even practice them in front of a mirror. I don't know.

It was just after lunch on a Saturday. She'd asked me and my sister, Marcy, and my brother, Robbie, to sit down on the couch.

We'd had peanut butter sandwiches for lunch. There were carrot sticks, too, but I don't like carrots. I'm actually pretty suspicious of them. So hard, so stiff, but they're a happy color, a bright bouncy orange. The color doesn't match what a carrot really *is*—cold, with that tough cover—and so I don't like them.

I won't eat carrots. I do, though, like peanut butter.

"I need to talk to you guys," my mother said.

Her name is Denise. She sells real estate, and on days when she's going out on sales calls and she dresses up, it's amazing. Suddenly our mother is not the same person at all anymore, not the person we know. She's this completely different person. She has blue eye shadow and mascara and blush, and heels and a navy blue pleated skirt and a white blouse and a jacket that matches the skirt. The jacket has gold buttons. She wears pearls with the outfit. Actually, she looks great.

Today she wasn't dressed up. She was wearing jeans and a sweatshirt that said *SOUTH CAROLINA: Life's a Beach!* She wears that sweatshirt all the time. I think it's her favorite. It's been washed so many times that the whole thing is about four shades lighter than the way it started out.

Somehow I knew, as soon as I heard what she was about to tell us, that the sweatshirt was the part I'd remember best. Even today, I can close my eyes and see it all again. The gray sweatshirt with the big saggy collar and the droopy sleeves. The slanty black letters. That exclamation point: *Life's a Beach!*

She was sitting in the big soft chair across from the couch. Right on the front edge of that chair. She'd dragged the chair closer to us, so that she could touch our knees as she spoke.

The lineup that faced her was: me, then Marcy, then Rob.

I was thirteen. Marcy was eight. Rob was four. For once in his life Robbie wasn't squirming, wasn't making a fuss. His hands were lying flat on the tops of his thighs. He looked oddly solemn and grown-up. Marcy fiddled with the flap of a small scab on her left elbow. I just waited.

"Listen, guys," my mother said. She always called us "guys." I could tell a speech was coming. "I got a call, okay? It was," she said, "from somebody in your dad's outfit." My mother, when she's nervous, has this singsong way of talking. "Things are really bad over there, and it's been a really scary time for us, right? It's been bad but we're doing fine because we love each other and we love your dad very, very, *very* much, don't we? And we know that God is looking out for him? And we say our prayers every night and hope he comes home soon?"

They weren't questions, exactly, but my mother was saying them like questions, the way teachers do when they want the lesson to just roll along without any interruption. When they've had the words planned, tucked away like tuna sandwiches and apple slices in a backpack, and they need to take them out in just the right order or the day will be ruined.

My mother wasn't crying. And she hadn't cried earlier, either, before she sat down and talked to us, because I would've been able to see it in her face. You can't hide crying. That's something you absolutely know by the time you're thirteen.

Marcy had stopped picking at that scab, but she was still looking at it, instead of looking at Mom.

Marcy didn't move. Neither did Rob. We were like three statues in the park.

"And we're going to be okay," Mom said. "Isn't that right? No matter what happens? Because we love each other? And we love Dad, right?"

I remember feeling a sour little trickle of dread, like that thing you get in the back of your throat when you know you're going to throw up.

I remember thinking, *Well, he's dead. That must be it. He must be dead, or she wouldn't be doing this. She wouldn't be talking to us this way.*

Already, I was going over in my mind just how I'd tell my friends, my teachers: *My dad is dead.* I didn't know anybody who had a parent who'd died. Lots of my friends had parents who were divorced or parents who had moved out. But not dead. Dead was different. I would get a lot of attention.

I realize that was a pretty awful thing to think. If my father was dead, I wasn't supposed to be thinking about myself or about feeling special. It was a terrible thing to be thinking. But that was what flashed across my mind. I thought about how Chris Brookhiser, this guy in my algebra class that I sort of liked, would look at me differently once he found out that my father had been killed in Iraq.

"Guys," my mother said, "we've got some very big changes ahead of us. Big, *big* changes, okay? But we'll get through it. Okay?"

The three statues did what statues do. Which is nothing. We just sat there.

And then she went back to speaking in a rush. The words seemed to tumble all over themselves, the way Robbie and his friends do when they're rolling down a hill, merging and blurring, three or four kids in one big squirmy ball.

"Guys, your dad and some other soldiers were in a terrible fight over there and there was a big explosion and some people were killed but your daddy wasn't killed—he's *alive*, he lived through it—and he's going to be coming home. But listen, I have to tell you—"

My mother stopped talking, but she still didn't cry. I think maybe she was afraid to. Once you start crying, sometimes you can't stop for a while, because crying works up its own momentum. And she had a lot to do, a lot of things to take care of. She always did.

"When your dad comes home," my mother went

on, "he's going to be different, okay? He was hurt really, really bad, and he—" She stopped. Then she went on.

There are things you hear that, once you hear them, just keep traveling through you forever, like sunlight through a windowpane. Like it's some sort of natural process. They don't stop. So you're never really *not* hearing them, ever again.

"He doesn't have one of his legs anymore," my mother said, "and he doesn't have one of his arms, either." She was saying these things in a strange calm voice like they were normal to say, like they were ordinary things. Like checking off items on a list for the store. "But he's going to be okay. He'll get better. They're going to give him a new leg and a new arm, and then he'll be able to get around and do things and play with you."

She touched Marcy's knee. Marcy was wearing shorts—Marcy almost always wears shorts, even in the wintertime—so it was bare skin that my mother touched. It was Mom's fingertips on Marcy's skin, just a simple bridge of bare skin. Skin to skin. "He'll be able to shoot baskets with you, sweetie," Mom said to Marcy. "The doctors told me that because I asked them. They'll teach him how to shoot a basketball with his new arm."

The three of us just looked at her. She didn't cry. So we didn't cry.

Life's a Beach! was what it said on her shirt. And after the words there was that exclamation point. The dot that made the bottom half of the exclamation point was colored like a beach ball, with red and white sections.

That's what I remember best: the red and the white. The little beach ball.

And the fact that nobody cried. Not then, anyway.

2. SLEEP

My name is Rachel Ann Browning. I *hate* my name. I've always hated it. To me, "Rachel" sort of sounds like a real snob, like somebody who thinks she's better than other people, but really isn't any better at all, and people will eventually find that out. *RACHEL ANN BROWNING.*

Right.

I wanted a nickname, and by fifth grade it had happened. Everybody started calling me "Brownie." I had to pretend I didn't like it, of course, because even way back then, I'd already figured out that if you show everybody that you're okay with a certain nickname, it's no fun for people to call you that name, and they'll stop. A nickname can start out as an insult, but it can end up as proof that you belong, that people have thought about you long enough to come up with another name for you. So at first you have to act all huffy and annoyed about it, even though you're secretly thrilled.

Pretty soon it caught on. "Brownie" was perfect for me.

And then, when I was still in fifth grade, my father told me that people had called *him* Brownie, too, when he was a kid. I didn't know that. It made me feel pretty good, the fact that a nickname had just sort of popped up on its own, all over again, as if it had been waiting around for somebody else in our family to take it over.

Dad told me that he hadn't liked his real name, either: Edward. So he got them to call him Brownie.

Just like me.

He didn't come home from the hospital right away. It was a long time, in fact, before we saw Dad again.

My mother went to Walter Reed Army Medical Center to visit him, but we didn't get to go. Aunt Belinda came to take care of us while Mom was away.

Belinda is my dad's oldest sister. She teaches chemistry at a community college in St. Louis.

The first few days with Aunt Belinda were rough. She doesn't have any kids, and so when she talked to us, it was like she wasn't quite sure of things. It was like she was feeling her way down a dark hallway with no idea where to look for the light switch.

"Bedtime's at eight," she said abruptly at breakfast one day. "Rachel can stay up until ten, but it's eight for you and Robbie," she added, looking at Marcy. She wanted, I think, to give us ground rules so we'd know what to expect. But you don't tell little kids like Robbie about bedtime the first thing in the morning. It's like you're erasing the whole day before it can even get started.

Robbie started to cry.

"Robbie, honey, don't cry—*please*," Belinda said. She jumped out of her chair. We were all sitting around the table, and there were brown sugar cinnamon Pop-Tarts, still too hot to eat, on paper plates in front of us.

She tried to pick up Robbie to hug him, but that was another mistake. He batted his arms at her as if she were a bumblebee. One of his small pinwheel palms caught her on the chin.

She stepped back, stunned.

"Rob!" Belinda said. "Robert! Goodness gracious!"

His crying got louder until it started to sound like a siren, which was not really a surprise. Marcy put her hands over her ears and slowly shook her head from side to side. There was no point in getting involved. I licked my finger and touched my Pop-Tart. Still too hot.

"Rob!" Belinda repeated. She was touching her chin, as if she couldn't believe he'd hit her—which he really hadn't, of course, because it was an accident, but when kids do things it always seems personal. On purpose.

Mom had left earlier that morning. One of our neighbors drove her to the airport. She had a two-hour flight to Washington, D.C., that left at eight a.m. Marcy and I counted it up: Eight o'clock, nine o'clock, ten o'clock.

Okay, then. She'd be seeing Dad a little after ten.

It was still just 8:12, according to the big clock on the kitchen wall, so we had a long time to go before

could safely take over and let the
... it in our minds: Mom and Dad, look-
... her. Him in a hospital bed, her standing
... ed.

... w what Dad would see. Mom had dressed
up for the trip. She was wearing nice blue slacks
and a white blouse. She'd ironed it the night before.
She was carrying a small red plaid suitcase. Plus her
purse.

But what would Mom see when she looked at Dad?

We didn't talk about it, but I knew that Marcy
couldn't imagine it, either. Couldn't think about our
father, with some pieces of him missing.

Aunt Belinda finally figured it out.

She realized that you can't try to hug Robbie when
he's upset, because you just make him more upset.
You have to let him cry sometimes. She'd set him off
by saying the word *bedtime* so early in the day—can
you really blame him?—and so she just had to deal
with the consequences. After that, she was fine.

We finished breakfast and moved into the living

room. Did anybody want to watch TV? Nope, nobody wanted to watch TV.

Marcy and I were on Christmas vacation from school. It was December 22. Our mother had had to wait a while before going to see Dad. First he was at a hospital in Germany, and then once he got back to the United States, she told us, he was still sleeping and so she waited to go visit him.

She called it "sleeping," but we knew what it really was: a coma. I knew, and then I told Marcy. She sort of knew what it meant, and she sort of didn't, too, so I explained it to her. We didn't tell Robbie.

Everybody asks me what Christmas was like that year. When your mother leaves just before Christmas Eve, and your father is in a hospital a long way away, and you really don't know what's going on or what's going to be happening to your family, what could Christmas be like?

The truth is: I don't remember.

I remember gray scraps and little bits of the days and nights, but I never put it all together in my head to make one whole memory. I don't think Marcy did, either. And Robbie didn't. We just lived through the time.

We had a tree. Aunt Belinda helped us put decorations on it, but it didn't feel like decorating a Christmas tree. It felt like hanging things on little branches. Usually when you're decorating the tree, the pine needles poke your fingertips and you say, *"Ow!"* and then you laugh, because it hurts but it doesn't hurt, both at the same time, but this time, with this tree, it just hurt.

We had hot chocolate on Christmas Eve, and then came Christmas morning.

I wish I could tell you more, but I just don't remember.

We lived through the time. That's all I know.

Mom called us every night. She was gone for five and a half weeks, and she called every night from the motel where she was staying.

The phone would ring, and Robbie and Marcy would fight each other to get there first. Sometimes, in the rush, they'd knock the phone off the hook, and then we'd hear a tiny version of Mom's voice that sounded like a cartoon voice—"Hello? Hi? Hey, anybody there?"—coming from the receiver down on the carpet.

If Belinda got to the phone first, she'd stand there and talk to Mom for a few minutes while we made a bobbing, frantic circle around her.

"How are you, Denise?" Belinda said into the phone. There was a pause. "I see." Another pause. "I see. Yes."

Belinda, who was tall and kind of skinny and had short, spiky silvery hair, was a careful speaker. A lot of teachers are careful speakers. They just naturally expect to be listened to, and so they are very picky about their words.

Robbie was always impatient. "Mommy!" he cried, clawing at Belinda's hip. "I want to talk to my mommy!"

Belinda reached down to stroke the top of his head while she kept on speaking into the receiver: "Yes. Yes, of course." She listened. "Oh, we're fine.

We're doing just great, hon, please don't worry. Can we do anything for you? Send you anything?"

I noticed that Belinda almost never asked about Dad. If you were listening to her and you didn't know what had happened, you wouldn't be able to figure it out from these talks. You wouldn't know why Mom was so far away from us. At Christmas, which is a weird time to be gone.

"Yes. Well, that sounds reasonable," Belinda said. "Right now, it's probably about the best we can expect, I suppose." Robbie was getting restless under her hand. "Denise, hon, I'd better let you talk to the kids. They're going crazy here." A pause. "Oh, no, really. It's no bother at all. It's been fun."

She looked at me and waggled her eyebrows. The part about it not being a bother was a private joke between us. She'd told me how hard it really was for her, being around small children like Robbie and Marcy. I knew how nervous they made her feel, with everything they needed all the time, and the crying and the mess. I could appreciate her problem, and I tried to help, but to tell you the truth, I had my own problems to deal with.

Belinda was used to college kids, kids who could take care of themselves. Right now, though, she was in charge of a couple of kids she didn't really understand. Kids who, in Robbie's case, still needed a glass of water at bedtime and a story. Marcy, too, could be a handful.

She let Robbie talk on the phone first. That, too, was a lesson she'd had to learn. The very first time Mom called, Belinda gave the phone to Marcy, without even thinking about it, and Robbie crumbled right before our eyes. He wanted to be first. His screams came so fast and the cries were so sharp that I don't think any of us would've been too surprised if he'd burst into flames and ended up a little pile of ashes.

"Mommy!" he yelled at the receiver.

I saw Belinda wince.

Robbie then began to babble into the phone in that annoying way that four-year-olds do, because they think they are definitely the center of the universe at all times. And *nothing* could be more important, could it, than the humongous Lego tower he'd built before he knocked it down, or the two and a half glasses of milk he'd had with his dinner, or the fact that Aunt Belinda had agreed to let him skip his bath that night if he *promised* to take one the next night?

He didn't ask about Dad. Marcy didn't ask, and when it was my turn to talk, I didn't ask, either.

Mom, though, brought it up with me. Her voice was way too bright, like a penny you find on the bottom of the pool. "Your father is doing very well," she said, during a call on one of those first few days after she'd gone away.

I nodded, even though I knew she couldn't see me.

"He's not talking yet," she added. "But he will."

"Okay," I said. I looked over at Marcy, who was watching me, and then up at Aunt Belinda, who wasn't; she was keeping an eye on Robbie, who, once he finished his turn talking on the phone, usually got distracted and just wandered off.

"Rachel, honey," Mom said. "Are you all right?"

"Yeah," I said. That's what I always said. It just made things easier.

"We'll be home soon, sweetheart."

A pause.

"Rachel, we're going to be okay," she said. "We'll get through this, okay?"

That was not the sort of sentence I wanted to hear. That was what you'd say to somebody a lot older than me—"getting through" and "going to be okay" were phrases from another world, from the adult world. They were bulky shapes with sheets thrown over them. It was hard to tell what they were really covering up. What was lurking underneath.

I didn't blame her for not knowing what to say. I felt sorry for her. Kids, I think, have a lot more reason to feel sorry for adults than adults have to feel sorry for kids. I know that sounds backwards. I know that's not how most people would see it. But here's the thing: kids know what they know. And that's it. Adults know all the things they *don't* know, all the questions and doubts and puzzles and darkness. Kids are all sealed up with the little bit they know. Adults, though, are leaking out all over the place, with everything they don't understand but think they should. I'll bet it gets pretty annoying.

This was right when I decided, for the time being, that I wasn't jealous of adults anymore, of all the freedom they have. I didn't want to be older, which was something I thought I wanted to be. I was glad to be thirteen. That was plenty for now.

"Oh," I said.

She asked me about our Christmas tree, and about the snow, and about my best friend Melanie Warrenton. Then, after she seemed to have run out of ways to fill up the silence, she asked about the fort in the backyard. "How is it doing," she asked, "with all the snow? How is it holding up?"

"It's fine," I said. "It's great."

Aunt Belinda's specialty was spaghetti.

The trouble was, though, Marcy was the only one who liked spaghetti. Robbie called it "worms and dirt." I couldn't even look at it sometimes. It always seemed to be moving on the plate. Wiggling. Which was disgusting.

At dinner, Belinda would try to get us to talk. It was hard. Our short answers must have seemed rude to her, but we just didn't have much to say. So she'd give up and tell us stories.

She'd known Dad as a child, and we were thrilled by her stories. Was he ever *really* that little—as little as Robbie is now? Did he *really* get locked in the basement once for five hours and nobody knew where he was until their dog Barney started barking like crazy by the basement door and somebody said, "The basement!" and they pulled open the stuck door and everybody ran down the stairs and they found him, and he wasn't even crying or scared, and then Dad's father—my grandfather, who died a long time ago—fixed the basement door so it wouldn't stick anymore when it closed behind you? That actually happened?

It happened, Belinda said. *Oh, yes.*

We loved the stories. Some of them we'd heard before, but a lot of them we hadn't.

There are times when you don't care about who your parents really are, or about where they came from. You want them to be your parents. That's it. All you care about is yourself. Your parents aren't real or important, except as far as they relate to you. And then there are times when you *do* care about who your parents are as real people. People out in the

JULIA KELLER

world. You care more than you can say. Right then we cared so much, and Belinda seemed to know that, without us having to say so.

I don't think we could have put it into words, anyway. But we did feel that way. So we listened.

Mom was gone for a long time.

We went back to school, me to eighth grade, Marcy to second. Rob was in half-day kindergarten. Belinda had to go back to her job in St. Louis, to her regular life, so our neighbors, Frank and Jessica Weber, came and stayed for the last two weeks before Mom came home.

The Webers didn't have any kids, either, so they could bring their stuff over to our house and settle in. They put their dog, a Labrador retriever named Otto, in a kennel because Marcy has allergies. Nobody was sure if Otto would make Marcy sneeze and cause her eyes to run all the time, but Frank said, "Why take the chance?"

Frank Weber is a big man with a happy smile and almost no hair left on the top of his head, just some wisps of brown, like scraps of paper that have gotten stuck up there. When he'd said, "Why take the chance?" he spread his hands out wide on either side of his body and shrugged, a really big sort of shrug that seemed to be happening in slow-motion. It was like somebody shrugging in a cartoon.

He did that with almost everything. You'd say, "What's for dinner, Frank?" and Frank Weber would say, "Hot dogs—anything wrong with that?" and the hands would go to both sides of his big body, palms up, and then there'd be the slow-motion shrug. And the smile. Or you'd say, "Can we stay up late tonight and watch TV?" and he'd say, "Why not?"

The spread-out hands, the big shrug. The smile. He was a nice guy. We liked him a lot.

We liked Jessica, too, but in a different way. She was much quieter than Frank. She was a tiny woman with a limp. Dad told us once, when we were first getting to know the Webers and they'd come over for dinner and then gone home, that she'd had an accident as a child and that was why she had the limp, but we weren't supposed to talk about it around her. We couldn't ask her about it, either. We weren't even supposed to notice it. But we all noticed it, of course. You couldn't help yourself.

So we spent most of our time around Jessica Weber pretending not to notice her limp. We kept our eyes on her eyes, which were small and black. She wore large black glasses.

"Why does Mrs. Weber walk like that?" Marcy asked me one day, when she was hanging out in my room and the Webers were in the kitchen making lunch. Ever since Mom had gone away to Walter Reed, I'd started to let Marcy hang out with me a little bit more. I didn't chase her out right away, which is what I used to do.

"Did Daddy ever tell you about Mrs. Weber's accident?" Marcy went on. "Like, what actually happened?"

We were thinking a lot about accidents. Mom was supposed to be coming home in a couple of days. We were doing fine with the Webers—they had not made spaghetti for dinner, not even once—but we were starting to want more information about all kinds of things.

"Nope," I said.

"What do you think it was?"

I shrugged. Not a Frank Weber kind of shrug—big, happy, with your shoulders going up slowly, slowly, like a roller-coaster car climbing the steepest part of the track and then dropping back down again with a whoosh.

It was just a regular old shrug, a quick one, to show her that I didn't really want to talk about it.

"But what do you think?" Marcy said.

"I don't think anything."

"But I *mean*—" Marcy stopped. I knew what she was thinking, almost as if I could see her brain doing its work. "I mean, was it an accident like Daddy's accident? I mean, Mrs. Weber is okay. She's fine. She goes kind of slow, but she's okay. If Daddy's accident was like Mrs. Weber's accident, that won't be bad at all."

I knew what she meant. I knew what she meant before she even told me what she meant.

And I still didn't want to talk about it.

Because I knew, a lot better than Marcy knew, that the word *accident* was not the kind of word you could count on. It wasn't a word that held its meaning. It changed. It shifted. It could be one thing in relation to one person; it could be something totally different in relation to another person.

Accident was just not a word you could ever trust. If you turned your back on it, it could trick you. I knew that whatever accident Mrs. Weber had had as a kid—when she walked these days, her right leg sort of lifted and spun around in a tiny circle before she took a step, then her left leg had to wait for that little spin and then she kind of lurched forward and straightened herself up again and got ready to take another step—it had nothing to do with how the words *accident* and *Dad* fit together. Nothing at all.

Mrs. Weber must have known that, too, because she never brought up the connection, never said to us, "Your father's going to be fine. Look at me—I had an accident a long time ago and I'm fine."

She never said that. But she really was fine. She worked in a bank.

Frank Weber was a finish carpenter and general handyman. He let Marcy play with his socket set. Because, he told her, there was nothing sharp in there that she could hurt herself with.

✝✝

Mom came home on a Sunday afternoon. It was January.

Our father did not come with her.

Time, she told us. "He needs more time. He's not ready yet."

I think she wanted to say, "And we're not ready yet, either."

But she didn't.

On February 17, we got a postcard in the mail. It had red squishy-looking hearts on it and was addressed to *THE BROWNING FAMILY*, with the address in big square letters that somebody had printed.

In the place on the postcard where you write the message, there were these words, also in big letters:

HAPPY VALENTINE'S DAY TO DENISE, RACHEL, MARCY, AND ROBBIE. LOVE,

And then, where the name of the person who sent the card ought to be, there was a squiggly line that curved down and right off the bottom of the card, as if the person who'd written it wasn't really paying attention. As if that person had maybe fallen asleep while he was writing his name, or maybe somebody had called for him and he had looked away from the place where he was writing.

Our mother made a big deal about the postcard.

"It's from your father!" she said. "Look, Rachel— it's Dad. That's his name there. See? Marcy, come on over here. Take a look! Robbie, honey, come here."

She was standing in the living room and we gathered around her. We took turns looking at the card and then passing it to the next person—me, Marcy, Robbie, Mom; me, Marcy, Robbie, Mom—and it went around the small circle several times.

When Marcy and I talked about it later, we agreed that it just looked like a scribble to us. Not somebody's name. It could have been anything, any word.

Robbie, though, didn't know how to read, anyway, so he seemed okay with it. He handed the postcard back up to Mom and he nodded, as if he'd seen all he needed to see.

"We ought to make a cake," Mom said. She was holding on to the postcard with both hands, even though it wasn't heavy. "For when your father gets home. What do you guys think?"

We thought: *Okay. A cake, then.*

"Not right away," she added. "I mean, we've still got some time. Another month or so, they say. Maybe a little longer. Then he'll be here. And then we'll make that cake, okay?"

Okay, we said. *Sure.*

On April 23, Dad came back.

3. POWER

We weren't there when they brought him in the house.

I say "brought him" because he couldn't walk by himself yet. He was in a wheelchair. He had a new leg, we knew. A leg that had been made especially for him and that you could take off and then snap back on.

We knew about the new leg because Mom had told us about it. She wanted us to know exactly what was going on, she said. All the details.

"No secrets," she said. There would be no secrets in this family. That was one of the ways we'd get through it: absolutely no secrets.

So we came in the house from school that afternoon, and we saw him, and you would think—because of all we'd been told, because nobody had lied to us about anything or held anything back—that we would not be surprised or afraid.

We would be totally ready.

You would naturally think that, wouldn't you?

Edward Jerome Browning Jr.

Sometimes, when I was a little kid and I was just learning to read, I'd find my father's name on an envelope or in a book or something, and in my mind, each word would seem to break off to become its own separate part, like a candy bar with those lines on it so that you can divide it into neat little pieces and share them with somebody:

Edward

Jerome

Browning

Jr.

By the time he got to be an adult, they didn't call him "Brownie" anymore. People called him "Eddie." Or "Ed." Mostly they called him "Ed," but the ones who knew him best, the friends who came by the house a lot and whose laughter always seemed to rhyme with my father's laughter, the laughter coming at the same time about the same things—well, those people called him "Eddie."

He was the public-relations director for Central States Consolidated Power Company. When the electricity went out—sometimes it happened in a storm, sometimes it just happened—Dad had to go down to the office. Sometimes he was there all night, all through the next day, and then the next night, too. He would come home and look very tired, and there would be big circles of sweat under the arms of his jacket and his hair would be sticking up and Mom would say, "Kids, just let your father get some sleep, okeydokey? That's what he needs."

Dad would grin at us and then sometimes give us a thumbs-up sign, too. It meant: *Sorry, guys. I'll be okay later.*

And he was. He'd sleep for a long time and when he woke up, he was back to his old self. "His old self." That was what Mom called it. Old self. Like you could have a different self for a little while, but your old self would always come back in the end.

Along with his older sister, Belinda, Dad also had

two younger brothers, Steve and Travis. Travis was an electrician. Steve didn't have a job. He hadn't had a job for a long time. I knew that because it was talked about whenever my father and Belinda talked on the phone.

They had all grown up in a big old house in St. Louis. Then Dad went away to college and he met my mother, and they got married and now, here we were. All of us.

I guess you would call us a normal family. Once a month, and sometimes other times, too, Dad would be gone for a few days. Mom told us that he was in the National Guard. We were normal, you could say.

And then we weren't.

I can still remember the day we heard the news: Dad was going to Iraq. His National Guard unit was being sent over there. After that, things moved pretty fast, so fast that there wasn't a lot of time to think about it or be scared about it. Before we knew it, he was gone.

At first, after he'd left for Iraq, it was like he was just on a regular trip somewhere. We got a lot of e-mails from him. Pictures, too.

We didn't watch the news on TV. Well, we did at the beginning, because Mom said we ought to keep up with the war so we'd be able to talk about it with Dad when he called or when we answered e-mails. It was our duty, she said. But then, when things started to get a whole lot worse over there, she asked us to please not watch the news anymore. I didn't argue with her. I didn't like watching the news, anyway.

And then, after we found out about Dad's accident, we had to learn a lot more new words, a whole rush of new words: *Comatose. Prosthesis. Aphasia. Dura mater. Frontal lobe. Subdural hematoma.*

It was mainly my mother and I who worked on the words, although at first Marcy said she wanted to learn them, too. I tried, but after a while, Marcy stopped asking me to explain them. I was glad. I didn't understand them all that well myself, and I think Marcy sort of caught on to that fact. Trying

to teach somebody something that you don't understand yourself is kind of pathetic, really.

Between the time when Dad got hurt and the
time when he came back home, the new words just
kept slamming into me, one after another. To tell you
the truth, having to learn the new words was kind of
annoying. Like having extra homework. Like being
punished for something we didn't even know we had
done. There were handbooks and pamphlets we were
supposed to "read and discuss."

And that wasn't all. I really wished people would
just quit trying so hard to "help us understand" or to
"prepare" us. To "soften the blow," as Travis said once
when he was visiting us right before Dad came back.

Travis and his wife Beth stayed for only an hour or
so that afternoon. Every time Beth looked at Robbie,
she started to cry. "It's just—" She sniffled, like she
had a bad cold. "It's just that—it's just—well, he just
looks *so much* like Eddie."

Uncle Travis shook his head. He sounded like
he wasn't too happy with her. "Beth, baby, come on.
They're just kids. You're freaking them out."

"But he *does*," Beth said. Her nose was red and wet.

A big fat tear wobbled on the end of one long black eyelash. I couldn't take my eyes off it. Then it fell and hit her cheek, and I could look away.

Mom left the room and came back with the coffeepot to put more coffee in their cups, even though their cups were still almost full, even though nobody had asked for more.

The day my father came back home was a school day. Marcy and I went to different buildings, but they were right next to each other, so when she didn't have basketball practice after school, we rode the same bus. Then we'd walk home from the bus stop. We never talked much.

Marcy and I came in the front door. We hadn't known exactly what day he was supposed to arrive, so this was a surprise. Dad was sitting in a wheelchair right there in the living room. The TV set was turned on. The sound was way too loud.

He was wearing a dark blue sweatshirt and black sweatpants with a double white stripe going down both legs.

Both legs.

But he only had one leg. And just one of his arms, even though you couldn't tell unless you looked at him really close. Before he came home, my mother had tried to talk with me about the situation, about what being an amputee meant and how they could make a prosthesis for an amputated limb, but I hadn't really listened. I think I believed that if I didn't listen, it wasn't real. I just nodded a lot. Now, I wished I'd listened to her. I wanted facts, and I wanted them fast.

Dad didn't look up at us. He was slumped over in the wheelchair. His good hand was curled on his lap. The other hand, the one I didn't want to think about, must have been tucked up into his sleeve. He looked like he was asleep.

The top of his head had these stiff little bristles coming out of it, like an old toothbrush. There were big bald patches, too. And a crooked purple line that looped around Dad's ear and then ran across the top of his head, like somebody had been kidding around with a crayon but wasn't really paying attention until things got out of hand.

Mom was sitting on the couch. She didn't get up when we came in. She just looked at us.

She smiled.

"Hey, guys," she said.

The room felt hot and stuffy, like a box with the lid left on too long. I thought for a minute that I actually couldn't breathe. I wanted to grab Marcy's hand, but I was the older sister. I couldn't do that. If there was any hand-grabbing, then Marcy was supposed to grab my hand, and I could help her, but I couldn't grab her hand first. I was thirteen. I knew what was expected of me.

Dad's head twitched. I saw the twitch and I felt it, too, as if somebody had poked me with a pair of scissors. I jerked. I couldn't help it.

But it was just a twitch. He still didn't lift his head to look at us.

"Girls," Mom said. "Come on in and sit down. How was school?"

Marcy didn't move, but she spoke first: "Where's Robbie?"

"Over at Jeff's," Mom said. Jeff Eggers, who lives a block and a half away, was just about Robbie's age.

"He's been there all day. I wanted you girls to have a chance to see your father first, without having to explain things to Robbie."

She patted the couch on either side of where she sat.

"Come on, girls," she said. "Come on over here and sit down and say hello." Her voice was careful and even. The words sounded stiff, like a new pair of shoes you've just brought home and you can tell, just by looking at them, that they're not going to fit right at first. Or maybe never.

It was all so weird. I wasn't sure anymore what the world was supposed to be like. I felt kind of sick to my stomach. My face was hot, like I'd been running. I wanted to sit down. I wanted to stand up. I wanted something to drink. I wanted something.

Marcy walked over to the couch and sat down. So I sat down, too. I was sort of mad that Marcy had gone first. I was the older sister.

Dad hadn't moved again since his head twitched. He still wasn't looking at us. He wasn't looking at anything, not even the TV set. He had a halfway-beard, a kind of sloppy dark thing that crawled up his cheeks and under his nose and down onto his neck.

His eyes were flat.

I couldn't look at his legs.

I couldn't even look at the arm he had left, the real arm.

I couldn't look at anything.

I don't know how long we all sat there without talking, that first afternoon.

The TV set kept making noise, the way TV sets do. They're like giant hoses that just keep running and running forever, unless somebody's willing to take charge of them and shut them off. You have to make a move to stop them. And nobody did.

Traumatic brain injury: more new vocabulary. Words Marcy and I had gotten used to saying. Before Dad came back, Mom had explained to us that those were the right words: *traumatic brain injury*. Not *brain damage*. If other people—like, say, the kids at school, or any of our teachers—used the phrase "brain damage," Mom had told us we were to correct them "gently but firmly."

Not "brain damage." Dad was not a "brain-damaged person," Mom said. He was "a person with a traumatic brain injury." Before Dad came back, she brought it up a lot. I wanted to roll my eyes at her—*Got it, Mom*—but I didn't. I let her go over it as many times as she wanted to.

I admit it: I was curious about exactly what had happened to my father. But I couldn't reveal that. Standing there in the living room that first day, staring at him but trying to pretend not to, I felt trapped and weird and kind of afraid, but also full of questions.

Later, Marcy asked me where they'd put his leg after they cut it off. Where had they taken it? And his arm, too. Exactly where was it now located? I acted like I was upset with her and her dumb questions, but I was wondering the same things myself. I just couldn't let Marcy see that.

The TV set was on so loud that I wasn't really sure what I was thinking—the sound kept drowning out my thoughts—but I could feel the questions growing inside me. I was starting to feel like I was Robbie's age again, like I was all questions, all the time. Nothing but questions. Unlike Robbie, though, I couldn't ask them out loud. I couldn't look stupid.

Where had they put his leg and his arm? Where had they stuck them? Were they stored somewhere, along with a bunch of other people's arms and legs, before they threw them all away? And if they threw them away, where did they throw them?

What if you found the box of thrown-out arms and legs? It would be incredibly gross. I had all kinds of questions that I knew I shouldn't be having, shouldn't be thinking, because they were so stupid— but I couldn't help myself. I wished like crazy that I was a kid again, just for a little while, so that I could ask some very basic questions and get away with it.

The TV set was turned to the channel that has Oprah Winfrey. People were laughing and clapping. Oprah was wearing a bright pink blouse and black pants and she was sitting on a couch. Each time she talked, the crowd would just start whooping and clapping, and then the camera would go to people's faces, faces opening up into huge smiles, like flowers blooming. I wondered if the sound from the TV was making Dad's head hurt, but it didn't seem to matter. He didn't seem to be paying attention to anything.

I had a sudden thought that just sort of took hold of me, the way somebody might grab your shoulder and not let go, even though you asked them to.

What if things were always going to be this way? What if, from now on, this was it? This was how our family was going to be. What if there was no turning back? No change. Nothing but this, going on and on and on.

I thought: I wouldn't be able to stand it.

Would I?

4. MOON

It was Melanie's idea to build the fort, I think, but once we started the actual construction, I was in charge. This was back in fourth grade. Melanie Warrenton was my best friend. It was just the two of us.

I knew exactly what I wanted in our fort. It was almost as if I'd always known, and the moment Melanie said we ought to build one, it just came to me. For the sides, we would use a bunch of old boards held up by sticks planted in the ground. We'd use a sheet of plywood for the roof.

The only thing we needed any help with was getting the sheet of plywood. Dad brought it and helped us make our roof.

I'm not sure how he knew that a sheet of plywood was exactly what we needed. I didn't talk about the fort in the house, not because it was a secret but because it just wasn't anybody else's business. But he knew, all the same.

On that Saturday morning a long time ago when Melanie and I were trying to finish the fort, I looked back toward our driveway and there was Dad, sliding a sheet of yellow plywood off the top of the car. He'd gone out to the hardware store and bought it, and then tied it to the roof of the car and brought it back.

He didn't say much to us. He didn't make a big deal about it. He just propped the plywood sheet up between the two walls we'd made, balancing it across them, and then he stood back.

"You've got to have a roof," he said. "For when it rains."

We nodded. We were quiet, not like kids at all just then but builders, serious people intent on serious matters. Melanie had her hands on her hips. She was filthy. There was dirt all over the knees of her pants from where she'd been scooting around on the ground, pushing the sticks in deeper and deeper to make the walls sturdier. Melanie had long thick dark hair that she wore in a ponytail that fell down her back.

I had short hair back then. I wiped at my face, which was caked with dirt, with the palms of my hands. I could feel the dirt on my chin and neck. There were little sticks and clumps of mud hanging off my pants, and more mud gripping my shoes. I felt great.

"Thanks, Dad," I said.

He nodded. He didn't break the spell by talking any more. It was as if he'd wanted to see a fort in the backyard, too, and was just waiting for us to build one, so that he could do something, could add something to it.

I knew he wouldn't hang around and bother us. He wasn't like that.

But he didn't leave right away, either. He put his hands on his hips, just like Melanie. I put my hands on my hips, too, and we just stood there, the three of us. We stared at the fort. A couple of stick walls, a dirt floor, a plywood roof. It looked like you could kick it over, if you wanted to. It didn't look strong enough to even last through the weekend.

The funny thing, though, is that it did last. We had to do some repairs from time to time, but it lasted. It lasted a long time, right up to the time when Dad came back from the war. And then it lasted on past that day, too. For a while.

I like remembering that day when we were standing there, me and Melanie Warrenton and Dad, looking at the fort. Three builders. No need to talk.

There are so many things I don't like to remember anymore. But this is a good thing to remember, that day at the new fort, because it's off by itself. It's not part of any other memory. It's just a fort. It's just a day. It's not heavy and sad, like other memories, like other things we had to remember after Dad came home, so that we would know how it had been before.

My room is at the back of the house. I could look out my window and see the fort. At night, if the moon was big enough and bright enough, and if there weren't too many clouds, I could look out the back window and see the fort so clearly. It almost gleamed.

I could see the stick walls, and that plywood roof,

as if it had been there forever, that fort, as if there had never been a time in the whole history of the world when there wasn't a fort out there, with a roof glowing yellow in the moonlight.

The first few days after Dad came back, it was like he wasn't really there. And that was okay.

It was like we were still secretly waiting for him to come home.

Because this wasn't him.

This was somebody we didn't know at all. It's probably good that he didn't look much like himself, because it was easier to pretend it wasn't him. Dad would be coming home later: that was what I told myself, when I thought about it.

My real dad was still gone. This guy—well, what could you say? He was somebody we didn't know. He was selfish. He couldn't talk right, so when he wanted something, he'd just start moaning or shouting, the way Robbie used to do if he hadn't had enough sleep the night before and you wouldn't let him have another Oreo.

We knew it was Dad. I mean, we weren't stupid or anything. It was just hard to think about for too long.

So I let the dream grow in my head, like a small tree I'd planted there. Like a secret tree. The tree was the idea that this wasn't Dad. The actual Dad was still back in Iraq.

The tree got taller in my mind. The leaves popped to life on the branches, soft and green and perfect. Dad was still over there, the true Dad, the real Dad. Dad with his legs and his arms. Dad was the person he'd always been and always would be. Sure, he'd stopped sending e-mails for a while, but he'd start up again as soon as he could. He was busy. You could understand that, couldn't you—how busy he was? He didn't have time to write, but he would. Soon.

The tree in my head was so big, it grew so fast, that it started to crowd out other things. But the other things were things I didn't really want to think about, anyway. So it was fine with me.

When Dad first came back, Robbie cried a lot. Dad scared him.

Robbie would slide past the wheelchair in the living room, and sometimes Dad would try to touch him. Robbie didn't mind the touching, I guess, but he didn't like being surprised.

Dad's good hand would flutter as he raised it up off the handrest on the wheelchair. It would move toward Robbie. Robbie would just start to cry.

Mom had to soothe both of them, Robbie and Dad. Both at once. She'd rub Robbie's shoulder and then she'd run a soft thumb under each of his eyes, to take care of the tears, and then she'd stroke Dad's arm — his good arm, the one he had left — and she'd say, "Okay, okay, okay," because Robbie was crying and Dad was making funny sounds in his throat. A kind of *uha-uha-uha-uha*. It was the kind of sound you'd make if you were lost and scared, and it wasn't just that you couldn't find your way back home — you also couldn't find the words to say that home was where you wanted to go.

So it was like you were lost twice.

You were double-lost.

The first few days were awful.

It got a little bit better, after a week or two.

But the first days—well, I'd like to say I can't remember them very well, like I can't remember that Christmas with Mom gone, but I do remember. You can't tell your memory what to do. You can't tell it what to keep and what to leave behind.

Believe me, I've tried.

At first, there were always people around the house. A physical therapist, another kind of therapist, a home-health-care aide. That's the way the guy introduced himself, as a "home-health-care aide," and it was such a long title that Marcy and I started saying it all the time to each other, and then we'd pile on more words and crack each other up: *Happy Hearty Healthy Home-Health-Care Aide from Alabama.* I know it sounds kind of silly, but I liked making Marcy laugh. Each time I added a word, she got even more tickled.

The home-health-care aide was named Joe. He got there a few days after Dad came back.

"Let's give it a shot, Ed, okay?" Joe said.

Joe was squatting down in front of Dad's wheel-chair. Dad wasn't looking at him. Dad almost never looked at you, and even when he did, you didn't know if he was really looking at you. Most of the time he'd just sit there, slumped over like a sack of potatoes, and he'd stare at the hand in his lap. His good hand.

The other hand, the phony one, the one made out of metal and wire, stayed on the handrest of the wheelchair.

Dad stared at his good hand.

Joe, though, was like some of the teachers I've had. He was funny and nice, and he didn't let you ignore him. Marcy and I liked to be there in the living room when Joe was working with Dad—that's what Mom called it, "working with Dad"—because he was so friendly and funny, no matter what Dad did. Or didn't do.

"Come on, Ed. Rise and shine, bud," Joe said.

He didn't really mean "rise." We found that out right away. He was just trying to get Dad to partici-pate. To look at him. Or look at anything, I guess.

"Come on, Eddie!" Joe said. "Let's see some

action, okay? You've got these beautiful girls right here, and they just want to see that handsome smile of yours. Can you smile at your girls, Ed? Can you do that?"

Marcy had giggled when Joe said "beautiful girls," which caused Joe to turn and look at her and give her a wide grin, which made her giggle harder, which made Joe smile even wider.

Then Joe turned back to Dad, who hadn't moved. My father's chin was still sunk in his chest, almost as if it had been glued there.

"Ed. Eddie, my man," said Joe.

Nothing.

"Ed, all we want is a smile, bud. Just one itty-bitty smile this morning, for your gorgeous girls over here," Joe said.

Because Joe was squatting like that in front of Dad, steadying himself by touching the front of each armrest on Dad's wheelchair, he was really close to Dad. He was too close. I got worried that if Dad jerked too quickly, which he did sometimes, he might accidentally bump Joe and knock him over.

Or maybe not so accidentally.

The thing is, there was something about Dad that was kind of mean. It seemed like a frustrated kind of meanness, not a meanness just to be mean. At least that's what I hoped it was. But he'd been home only a little while and already I'd gotten glimpses of this dark, angry part of him that would just flare up, like a lit match. Maybe it had been there all the time, but he'd cared enough before this to keep it hidden. Maybe there's some meanness in everybody. I didn't think that before, but I do now.

"Eddie! Ed, come on," Joe said. "One teensy-weensy little smile. You want these young ladies here to see you smile, right? You want to show 'em you're a-okay? You don't want 'em worrying about their old dad, right?"

Nothing.

Joe shifted around a bit, still holding on to the front of the wheelchair. It must've been hard to squat like that, I thought. Joe was a skinny guy, with short blond hair and a big nose and a little beard that looped around his mouth in a fuzzy *O* that made him look like he was always surprised at something. He wore tight brown pants and white tennis shoes and a tight green T-shirt that said, IF IT'S PHYSICAL, IT'S THERAPY. He was skinny, like I said, but he had big hands.

And he never seemed to give up. Ever. That first day he was in our house, right after Dad came back, he tried again and again and again to get Dad to look up. It didn't work, but Joe kept trying.

Joe didn't seem to mind that Dad was ignoring him. I would've gotten mad. It would've hurt my feelings. But not Joe. He just tilted his head, grinned, and kept going. He peered at my father as if he thought Dad was just kidding around and really did want to talk to us.

"Come on, Ed! Rise and shine, bro. We've got a big day ahead. Sun's out. Spring's in the air."

Nothing.

Joe would sometimes wheel Dad out onto the back patio just off the kitchen. Joe would stand behind Dad's chair and fold his arms across his chest and just stand there with a big goofy smile on his face, as if he, Joe, had personally made all of what they saw, had dreamed it up it just a couple of hours before: trees, sun, sky. "There you go, bro!" Joe said. "Pretty cool, right? Take at look at the world. Take a look at all that. Not too shabby!"

My father didn't raise his head, but he muttered something. His muttering always sounded like some-body arguing, but nobody was arguing with him. It was a noise that could confuse you.

Marcy and I were standing in the kitchen, watch-ing. Joe had left the screen door open. So we were watching Joe, and Joe was watching Dad, and Dad— well, nobody knew what Dad was watching, I guess. If he was watching anything.

Mom was out on a sales call. Even though Dad had just gotten back, Mom said she had to go to work, and that morning, she had asked Joe if it was okay if she left while he was there.

I knew what she meant. Joe knew, too. He'd be taking care of Dad, but he'd also be keeping an eye on us. Robbie was over at Jeff's.

While Dad was in Iraq, my mother had left Marcy and me by ourselves lots of times. I was in charge. No problem. But when Dad came back home, that changed. It wasn't like she didn't trust me anymore. It wasn't that at all. She just seemed more fearful than I'd ever known her to be. Apprehensive, I guess you'd call it. Not about anything specific, not about any actual danger, but about everything in general.

"Sure, absolutely," Joe said. "No problem." As he said it, he'd given Marcy one of those big grins of his, the kind that made you wonder how his mouth could stretch that much past its normal shape and then get back to where it was in the first place.

Mom thanked him and then she left. She was dressed up. She had to go to work. I knew she was really worried about money. She'd told us about that. Plus, I had heard her on the phone with Aunt Belinda, talking about money, even before Dad came back.

While Dad was in Iraq, he'd gotten his army pay and most of the salary from his regular job, too. And once he was back, there was insurance. But I knew Mom was worried about the future, about all the medical bills and everything else. "We have to be careful now," was how she'd put it to me. She didn't talk about it with Marcy or Robbie. Just me. "We have to be very, very careful about money," she said, "because we just don't know how things are going to turn out." I wanted to say: *Well, that's always kind of true, isn't it? Nobody knows the future.* But I didn't say that because I didn't want to sound argumentative.

So she left for a while that day. And Marcy and I watched Joe work.

He explained to us that he wasn't a physical therapist or an occupational therapist, although he hoped to go to physical-therapy school one day. He was a home-health-care aide. He came to people's houses after they'd been sick or had accidents, and helped them take a shower or learn how to climb stairs or button a shirt or make a pot of coffee. Small things.

"Small things are big things," Joe said.

One of the people he'd worked with, Joe told us, called him "Shower Man." That was what he'd called him. Not "Joe." Not "Mr. Salisbury." Just "Shower Man."

And so, Joe said, he'd started thinking of a superhero called Shower Man. A guy who went around the world cleaning up people who couldn't do it themselves right then, and by doing that, he defeated the evil Dirt Monster. Or the Dirt Monster's cousin, the Lazy Monster, who kept people from doing all the things they ought to be doing to get better.

Shower Man was brave. Shower Man was loyal. Shower Man's outfit would be—well, what? Maybe a shower cap and a bathrobe and a pair of flip-flops. Maybe a toilet-bowl brush instead of a sword.

This made Marcy laugh. I laughed, too, but not as hard as Marcy did. She really liked Joe. I could tell.

He told us the Shower Man story while he was wheeling Dad back inside the house that day.

Dad's good arm was fluttering a lot. It shook and shook, and I thought it was pretty scary to see. But it didn't bother Joe at all.

He put Dad's wheelchair back in the middle of the living room, facing the couch. Marcy sat down on the couch. I went over and stood by the window. I don't know why. I didn't want to look outside or anything. I just didn't want to sit down on the couch right then, facing my father.

Joe was checking off some things on a notepad. Then he stuffed the notepad in his back pocket. He stuck the pen behind his right ear.

He kneeled down beside Dad's wheelchair.

"Okay, Ed," he said. "I'm going to let you slide for today, buddy. Just this once. I'm not even going to haul your butt into the shower or give you a shave. Doesn't seem like a good idea today. You're just not getting with the program today, my man."

Marcy giggled when Joe said the word *butt*, and he turned and winked at her.

I was getting a little irritated with Marcy. It was like she'd forgotten all about Dad. It was like Dad was not even there, and only Joe mattered.

"When your pretty little wife gets back, Ed, I'm taking off," Joe said. "But next time—look out. It's Shower Man. Shower Man's here. It's Shower Man to the rescue!"

His voice swooped up and up, like he was on a TV show or something, and Marcy laughed. I wanted to laugh, too, but I didn't, because I was mad at her.

I was mad at everything.

They'd taken him somewhere.

It was as if they'd taken Dad somewhere else and left him there. They pretended that they'd brought him back but they really hadn't.

It wasn't him.

It was this man in black sweatpants and a sweat-shirt. A man none of us knew. With no hair. And no emotions — or sometimes, with too many emotions, like when he'd groan and rock back and forth, getting upset about something. Or about nothing.

He was supposed to know how to go to the bathroom by himself. They'd taught him that in the hospital, Mom said. But he really couldn't. Or didn't want to. Because he would pee on himself sometimes. Was he doing it on purpose? Maybe, I thought. Maybe he was. But who'd want to pee on themselves?

You could smell it if you were walking by his wheelchair. You could act like you didn't smell it, but you did. You couldn't help it.

He was supposed to know how to take care of himself. He had a new leg and a new arm. He had been taught in the hospital — Mom told us, and Joe told us, too — how to "attend to his personal needs." That was what they called it, both of them, at separate times, which meant they had gotten it off a sheet of paper.

It meant things like going to the bathroom. Peeing and pooping. You wouldn't normally talk about those things—Mom made that very clear, especially to Robbie—except that sometimes you had to, like now. It wasn't embarrassing to talk about when you had to talk about it. It was, Mom said, "just part of life."

Peeing and pooping. You can't get around it. You've got to poop and pee, Joe told us, and while naturally we wanted to laugh when he talked that way, we didn't. Joe explained that we'd have to learn to talk about it without giggling because, well, it's life. It's the nature of life.

That's how Joe put it, even though he must've known that I was way too old to have this explained to me. You have waste products in your body and they have to come out, he said. Otherwise, it's like keeping poison inside your body. It's like garbage in a house. Can you imagine, he said, a house where they never took the garbage out? Where it stacked up for days and days?

"Stinky!" Marcy called out, as if she was in school and wanted to impress the teacher. "*Real* stinky!"

Joe nodded. He'd just come out of our parents' bedroom, where he'd wheeled Dad so he could clean him up.

Dad's wheelchair wouldn't fit very well into the bathroom yet. Uncle Steve and Uncle Travis were going to work on widening the door, Mom said. They had plans to do that. But for now, when Joe needed to clean up Dad in private, he'd take him into Mom and Dad's bedroom, and when he wheeled him back out, Dad didn't smell like pee anymore. Until later, when the whole thing happened again.

Dad was supposed to be doing a lot more things on his own. Even though he'd just been home for a little while.

They'd gone over it all in the hospital, Joe told us. They would've gone over it again and again, day after day. They would've shown him how to get from the wheelchair using his good arm, and they would've told him that soon he'd be able to use the other arm just as much, and they would've shown him how to walk with his artificial leg.

Artificial. What a weird word, when used about a part of your body.

Dad knew how to get up and move around on his

artificial leg, Joe said. And to use his artificial arm. They'd taught him how to do that.

He knew how to do it.

He knew. Which meant that when he didn't do it, it was because he really didn't want to.

That was how I thought about it, anyway, until I started to understand. It's not that Dad didn't want to do things. It's that the part of his brain that told him to do things was one of the parts that was injured. So what looked like laziness wasn't laziness at all. When it looked like he just didn't care, it wasn't that he didn't care.

Caring, it turns out, comes from your brain. I know that's a strange way to think about it, but it's true: caring comes from your brain. The part of my father that wanted to do things wasn't there anymore. He needed us to do his caring for him now.

Dad was depressed, Mom told us.

Joe had used the same word: *depressed*.

Mom was sitting at the kitchen table with Marcy and me one day, having lunch. Our father was sleeping.

He slept a lot. Joe wasn't scheduled to come that day, so Mom hadn't dressed Dad that morning. He was still in his pajamas. It was always a struggle to get him dressed, to fit his arms in a T-shirt and jam his legs in sweatpants; he fussed and he flailed, and once he had accidentally whacked Mom on the cheek, leaving a red welt. So if nobody was coming by to work with him on a particular day, Mom just didn't do it. It was one less hassle. She asked us, though, not to tell Joe that she let Dad stay in his pajamas all day.

"He's depressed," Mom said, "and that's why he just sits there. That's what they told me in the hospital, and that's what Joe says, too. But he won't always be this way. He won't always be depressed."

Marcy nodded. Because Mom had mentioned Joe, Marcy was satisfied with the explanation. She pretended that she understood.

I think I nodded, too, but not because I understood. I just wanted everybody to stop talking about it for a while.

After about a month, Joe told us that he wouldn't be coming back anymore. It turned out that you only got a home-health-care aide for a certain period of time. You were supposed to get to where you didn't need the help anymore.

That's what was supposed to happen: progress.

The physical therapist would still come by, Joe said. And pretty soon, when Dad started getting around better, he'd go to a rehab center several times a week to learn how to walk even better with his new leg. Pretty soon, Joe said, Dad would walk so smoothly that nobody would even know he didn't still have his own leg. It was just a matter of time.

But you only got a home-health-care aide for so long. And Joe's time was up.

He kneeled down in front of Dad's wheelchair and tried to look him in the eye.

"Hey, Ed. This is it, bud," Joe said.

Marcy was standing on one side of Dad's wheelchair. I was on the other. Mom was standing behind the chair.

It was a Thursday afternoon. Joe was supposed to

have left already, but he'd waited for me and Marcy to get home from school.

Dad moved in his wheelchair, moved his shoulders just a little bit. I guess it was his way of saying good-bye to Joe. Or maybe he just needed to move his shoulders. I don't know. There's no way for me to know. But it seemed like maybe it was a good-bye. Or maybe that's just what we wanted it to be, so that's how we saw it.

"Okay, bud," Joe said. "I'm outta here." He stood up. When he was squatting down in front of Dad's wheelchair, which he did a lot, I forgot how tall Joe really was. He was a tall man. Not as tall as Dad, but tall.

Joe hugged our mother. He shook Marcy's hand. He shook my hand, too.

I kept waiting for him to say something like "Good luck" or "Keep in touch," but he didn't.

I figured out later, after we'd had a whole bunch of Joes come through our house, so many Joes that you lost track and usually forgot their names, that he didn't say those things because he knew they didn't matter. He wouldn't keep in touch. Why say the words?

There would be another Joe, and another and another. There would be people who came to help. Strangers who were paid to help us, who entered our lives for a while and then left to make way for other strangers, and the only thing that stayed the same was Dad. He was the still point in the center, sitting there in his wheelchair, while everything happened around him, circling, whirling, changing.

Maybe Dad had it right all along: Why get involved? Why look them in the eye, when you'd just be looking into another pair of eyes a little bit later down the road, and another, and another?

At somebody else squatting down in front of you, saying bright, hopeful things you didn't actually have to believe in order to say?

Or helping you to shower and shave? Or wiping the pee off your leg?

I don't know if Dad ever felt like that. But I sure did.

Marcy was upset at first, after Joe left us. But then there was Ken, the occupational therapist. And

Barbara, the speech therapist, who liked basketball just as much as Marcy did. That's what she told Marcy, anyway, the first day we met her.

Pretty soon, Joe was just somebody who'd been around the house right after Dad came back.

There were a lot of people like that. They'd come and they'd go.

Dad just sat there.

I asked Marcy about Joe. A couple of weeks after he'd left us, I said, "You remember Joe, right?"

Marcy shrugged.

"Shower Man," she said, and that was it. That was all she said, only there wasn't any swoop to her voice. It was flat. As if she was making fun of herself, of how much she'd liked Joe. "Shower Man," she said. "Shower Man to the rescue."

5. STAR

School was weird. People—teachers, other kids, our friends—treated us like we were made of paper or something, and if they said the wrong thing, or even if they said the right thing in the wrong way, it would be like poking a finger through a thin sheet of paper. You'd tear the paper, leave a hole, even if you didn't mean to.

So walking through the halls at school could be like walking through a ghost town. People were all around us, we could see them and hear them, but just barely. We'd pass kids in the hall and they'd sort of drift away from us, not like they hated us or anything but like they didn't know what to do, what to say, so it made them want to keep their distance.

"Keep their distance." It was a phrase I'd never really thought much about, but when I did, I realized it was perfect. Distance was something you could say was yours, like a backpack or a flashlight. Deciding just to stay away from somebody was a thing you could hold on to, just like any other kind of thing.

My class had talked about Iraq, even before Dad went there. My World History teacher, Mrs. McGill, had a big map and asked us where it was. I was the only one in the class who knew where it was, before she showed us, because Dad had pointed it out to us on a map at home. When the war started, he showed us. He said everybody ought to know.

And then Dad was sent to Iraq. I was the only one in my class who had a parent who was there.

At first it made me feel special: *My dad is a soldier in Iraq*. He wasn't really a soldier, though, he'd told us. He said he wasn't like the guys who did it full-time. He worked at Consolidated Power. ConPow, everybody called it. That was his real job. But for while he was a soldier. For a little while, he was.

Then he came back. Maybe he hadn't been a real soldier, like somebody who's done that job for a long time and it's their only job, but he'd gotten hurt the same way the real soldiers do.

After a while, Mrs. McGill stopped talking about Iraq, or the war. She put the map away.

Marcy's class had never talked about it at all. Second grade was too soon, I guess, to know about the world.

I don't know how the teachers or the other kids or Mrs. Frye, the principal, found out about Dad's accident. We didn't talk about it. It was on the TV news in our town, but just twice, and not for very long: the first time was when Dad first came back, and the second time was a couple of months later when there was a primary election coming up and somebody running for Congress wanted to have his picture taken with Dad. The man running for Congress thought Dad was a good example of what happens when you're fighting in an "immoral war." That's what he kept calling it.

Mom wouldn't let him come by and get his picture taken with Dad. He must've called the local TV news and told them about it, because the next thing we knew, somebody from the TV station called and asked Mom about the picture. Why wouldn't she let the man get his picture taken with Dad? So that was the second story about our father that was on TV: "I DON'T KNOW WHY!" Mom had yelled at the reporter on the phone.

They had it on tape. They had taped the call with her, then they played the tape on the news. The picture on the screen was a picture from the day Dad came back, when they were unloading his wheelchair from the van and Mom was standing there in the driveway in her navy blue skirt and matching jacket and white blouse. On the TV news, Mom's voice in the taped phone call was angry. She was breathing hard: *"I don't know why I don't care please go away please leave us alone please please please."*

The person from the TV station had kept on asking her about the "immoral war" part, and about the man running for Congress, and Mom just kept saying, *"Please please please please please,"* until they finally gave up.

But they put it on the news, anyway.

So maybe that's how people at school found out about Dad. All I knew was, I didn't have to explain anything. They already knew.

I was off the hook.

One day, Mrs. Cuthbertson, our English teacher, asked us to write about ourselves. "Pretend," she said, "that you're a character in a short story. How would you describe yourself? Which words would you use? What would you say?"

I wrote down some things. I kept it pretty vague. But later, when I was at home in my room, I wrote down more things. Just for myself. I made my own list.

Here is what I wrote:

Brown hair.

Green eyes.

Glasses.

Three small moles on the left side of my neck.

A scar on my right knee, where I fell off my bike when I was ten and went skidding across the driveway. It bled a lot. I cried, but I was younger then. Not like now. I wouldn't cry now.

My favorite food is probably pizza.

I used to read a lot of books—*A Wrinkle in Time* was my favorite—but not so much anymore. I still have my copy of *A Wrinkle in Time*, though. I like to see it there on the shelf beside my bed.

My favorite subject in school is science.

I don't have a boyfriend, because I don't want a boyfriend.

I used to play a lot of soccer, but not anymore. And I never cared about it the way Marcy cares about basketball. Marcy is *obsessed* with basketball.

My hair is short and way too curly. It's hard to comb, especially after I wash it. Mom bought me something called "Curl Relaxer." The name made me laugh. I could picture my hair going crazy—springing out all over the place—and then this deep voice saying, "Just *relax*. Settle down. *R-e-l-a-x* . . . ," like the voice on a mattress commercial on TV.

I don't know what I want to be when I grow up. Probably an engineer.

My mother sometimes says I am too smart for my own good. And that I am "stubborn as the day is long." She says Robbie is stubborn that way, too. She says it comes from Dad's side of the family.

And then she laughs, because if one of us has a good quality, she always says it's from her side of the family, but if it's something annoying, she blames Dad's family. It's her way of teasing.

The hardest part about school, after Dad came back, was being with my friends. That's because I knew they wanted to ask me questions about Dad. But they didn't.

Maybe their parents told them not to. I don't know. But sometimes we'd be in the cafeteria, or getting stuff out of our lockers, or just hanging out, and there would be this funny silence. It would come from out of nowhere. First, we'd all be talking and laughing, like we always did, and then the silence would just drop in our laps. *Boom*. Right in the middle of things.

On Saturdays, Melanie and Susan Jessup and I usually went to the mall. It was just what we did. We'd walk around and, in whispers that were a lot louder than actual whispers, we'd make fun of people's outfits. Then we'd get makeovers at the cosmetics counter at Nordstrom. Sometimes we went to a movie later on. Then we'd go to Taco Bell. There was a Taco Bell right by the mall.

Melanie and I had been best friends for as long as I could remember. Susan Jessup came along later, in sixth grade. Her family moved here from Baltimore. She was okay. I didn't like her as much as I liked Melanie, but Melanie liked her a lot, so that was how it was: if I wanted to stay friends with Melanie, I had to include Susan Jessup in all the stuff Melanie and I did. The older I got, the more I learned about bargains.

It used to be that Melanie and I would make a plan, and then we'd call Susan. But after Dad came back, things were different. Susan Jessup would call Melanie, and they'd make a plan, and then they would call me and ask if I wanted to come along. Sometimes, I knew, they didn't call me.

One Saturday, we were all set to go to the mall. Susan and Melanie were supposed to come over to my house, and then my mother would drive us over there. She had a house to show in that direction, anyway.

But it turned out to be a bad morning. Dad wouldn't get out of bed, and Mom got very upset. She started yelling at him. They were back in the bedroom, but you could still hear her all over the house: "For *Christ's sake*, Eddie, it's eleven o'clock in the morning! I can't leave if you're still in bed. I *have* to get you up. Eddie, Eddie—come *on*. Get *up*."

I stood in the living room. Melanie and Susan were there, too. They had just gotten dropped off by their moms. Everybody could hear everything. We were completely still, like we were frozen by embarrassment, the three of us with our jackets all zipped up, ready to go, with the straps of our purses already arranged on our shoulders.

Nobody looked at anybody else.

Mom's voice was getting louder: "Eddie, I'm taking Rachel and her friends to the mall. And I've got a showing. I have to *go*, Eddie, I have to *leave*. Okay? But first you've got to get up. You have to go to the bathroom, okay? Okay?"

And then she must've lowered her voice, because we didn't hear anything else. We just went on standing there. Then there was the sound of a flushing toilet. The fact that we could hear it, way out in the living room, meant that Mom hadn't shut the bathroom door after she'd helped Dad go in there. We could hear everything.

Melanie looked over at me. Quickly. Just for a second, or maybe less. She had the funniest look on her face. It wasn't pity, exactly. It wasn't sympathy, either. It was like a question. It was like she was asking me, "How do you stand this?" but she wasn't asking me with words.

And it was pretty soon after that day, if I had to pick a time, that she and Susan started to do more things together, without asking me to come along.

That was fine with me. Really, I didn't care.

I was tired of going to the mall, anyway. I had a lot better things to do than walk around the mall.

When Dad was over in Iraq, he sent us e-mails and pictures. We kept them all.

I loved the pictures. There were pictures of him with his friends. There was a friend named Sam, who had his shirt off in a lot of the pictures, and another friend named Amy, who wore sunglasses all the time, and two other friends named Rafael and Clyde.

Dad didn't know any of these people before he went to Iraq.

The background in these pictures is mostly white and light brown and light yellow. The sky seems to go on and on, like one of those dreams you have that you can't get out of. You try to wake up and shake yourself free of the dream, but it's like a spiderweb. It's sticky and it clings to you. You're stuck in it. Not always in a bad way—you don't feel desperate or scared. Just kind of annoyed. It's not like a nightmare. It's just a dream that won't let go.

A dream that hasn't gotten the message that it's morning now. That it's supposed to move on.

The sky in Dad's pictures from Iraq looked like that to me: like a dream that lasts too long.

It was whitish-yellow, and it was always hanging around while Dad and his friends grinned and made funny faces in front of the camera. The too-long dream spread out over their heads.

Clyde, in the pictures, shows his muscles. He holds up his right arm. He's wearing an army T-shirt and a funny floppy hat. He has a big fat muscle in his arm and he points to it with his left hand.

Sam almost always has a cigarette hanging out of his mouth, like it's just another part of his body.

When you look at pictures of Sam, you think: *Is that a picture of Sam or a picture of a cigarette?* The cigarette always seemed to be right in the center of everything, slanting out of Sam's mouth, white against his black skin.

There are big trucks in the pictures. And tents. And dirt roads that look like they don't really go anywhere.

There are pictures of some of the kids in Iraq. They look right at the camera and they are smiling. They seem shy. Their clothes are funny. Their hair is dark and shiny. So black, it looks blue. Their eyes remind me of small black rocks you find in the creek sometimes, rocks that have been rinsed by the water so many times, over and over again, just because of being there in the creek, that they gleam. If you wanted to, you could say their eyes were beautiful.

But in the background of the pictures Dad sent is that sky, that sticky dream of a sky that looks like it wants to hold you there forever.

There it is, in the pictures of Dad and his friends. There it is, in the pictures of Rafael, and of Sam with his cigarette, and of Amy and Clyde, and of

Dad washing his shirt in a sink, and of the Iraqi kids, and of the dusty towns, and of the roads that go nowhere.

Dad sent us pictures and in these pictures is the sky. You can't get away from it.

Sometimes, just before I fell asleep at night, I wondered: *If you took a picture of my father or anybody else who'd been to Iraq, if you took a picture of them once they were back, would you still see that white-yellow sky?*

Even though they're home now, you might see that sky again, sneaking back into the picture. As if it was maybe saying, *Well, you thought you left me behind, but no, look. I'm still here.*

Wherever you go, maybe that sky goes, too. White. And yellow. And light brown. And so much like a dream, a dream that just doesn't know when to quit.

6. HUMVEE

Dad never told us about the accident.

"He doesn't remember it," Aunt Belinda said. Uncle Travis told us the same thing, and so did Dr. Vance, who came by the house a few times to talk to us.

Dr. Vance was, she told us, a psychotherapist.

Every time I write that word, I have to check the spelling. I can't get the first four or five letters straight. I almost always mess them up. I put the *s* where the *y* ought to go, and to tell you the truth, starting the whole thing out with a *p* makes no sense to me at all.

Dr. Vance was part of Dad's home-health-care team. Joe told us it was called a "home-health-care team," which made Marcy giggle, because the only teams she'd ever heard of were basketball teams and football teams and soccer teams. Dr. Vance visited our house three times.

She was there once right before Dad came home from the hospital in Washington. Then she came twice after he was back, to see how we were doing, I guess.

Dr. Vance had short dark hair and glasses and was very polite to us. Robbie hated her. He does that: if he doesn't like somebody right away, he just doesn't like them, and that's that. He never changes his mind. I think that's the stubbornness Mom is always talking about.

Dr. Vance sat on the couch. She wore white pants and a tucked-in pink blouse and a gold necklace. Her glasses were red and round. Mom offered her some iced tea or maybe a glass of water but she said, "No thank you, Mrs. Browning, I'm just fine, thanks."

And then she smiled. It was an automatic smile, like something she always kept handy in her purse and took out whenever she needed to, like a Kleenex or a cinnamon mint.

Dad was probably going to come home in a couple of days, Dr. Vance told us.

"We just wanted to make sure," she said, "that everybody's on board with what's going to be happening. He's made a lot of progress, but there's still a long way to go."

We just sat there.

We didn't know this woman.

She knew things about Dad that we didn't know, but he was our father. So it felt weird to have this stranger telling us things about him.

Dr. Vance let the silence go on. It was as if somebody had spilled something on the floor, and instead of cleaning it up, we all just watched the silence spread.

You could believe that Dr. Vance was counting off the seconds, that she'd been taught just how long to let the silence widen out in the room before doing something about it.

"So," she said. "I know the other members of the home-health-care team have been by to check on the adequacy of the facilities—" She stopped and gave us a small smile. "That means things like steps, and bathroom access." She honed in on Robbie, who was sitting on the floor, watching her the way you'd watch an interesting new kind of bug. "Your father is going to need a lot of help at first, but then he'll get better and be able to take good care of himself."

Robbie started to cry. Just like that.

Dr. Vance leaned back. She looked surprised. Mom immediately stood up and went over and sat down on the floor next to Robbie. She gathered up all the parts of him in her arms like stray flowers that she'd somehow dropped and needed to put back together right away to restore the most beautiful bouquet in the world.

"I'm sorry," Dr. Vance said. "Did I—?"

"It's okay," Mommy told her. "Please go on." She kissed the top of Robbie's head. Once, twice. His crying had turned into whimpers.

Dr. Vance hesitated, but then continued. "Well, I was just saying that, given the extent and severity of Mr. Browning's injuries, he's really been making good progress. He'll need a lot of help at first, but over time, he'll become more independent. Especially once he gets used to his prosthetic leg."

Prosthetic. Prosthesis. Those words again. Hard to say, hard to spell. Hard to like.

"That's not part of my job, though," Dr. Vance said. "We have plenty of other people who will deal with Mr. Browning's physical needs. I'm here to talk about how everybody's feeling."

She waited. I guess she expected somebody to start talking.

But nobody did.

Dr. Vance knew her stuff. Instead of waiting for us—believe me, if she'd done that, we'd all still be sitting there—she called us by name and aimed specific questions at each person.

"Okay, well then, let me ask you, Marcy," Dr. Vance said, turning to my sister, who sat beside her on the couch. "You're in second grade, right?"

Marcy nodded.

"Do you understand what happened to your father?"

Another nod.

"And what was that?"

Marcy looked at Mom, who smiled at her, and then Marcy said, "He was a soldier. He got hurt."

"That's right, sweetheart," Dr. Vance said.

I knew my turn was coming, so I was ready for her. I was sitting on a chair that I'd dragged in from the kitchen, because we didn't have enough seats in the living room for everybody.

"Rachel," Dr. Vance said. Her voice wasn't as soft and soothing as it had been when she was talking to Marcy. And I could tell Dr. Vance thought this was a compliment. She could talk to me the way one adult talked to another adult. "How are you?"

"I'm okay."

"Why don't you tell me how you feel about your father and what happened to him."

I waited. I already knew exactly what I wanted to say, but I didn't want her to know that. I wanted her to think it was just coming out of me. That I hadn't thought about it until just this minute.

"I sort of wish," I said, "that everybody would leave us alone. I want Dad to come home and everything to be back the way it was."

Dr. Vance nodded, as if she'd known everything I was going to say before I said it. Which was really annoying. But I couldn't show that I was mad, because she probably expected that, too.

"Well," she said, "we'd all love for things to be how they were. But your father is a brave man and he was serving his country. He got hurt. He's going to seem different to you, at first. But the thing I want you to remember—" Dr. Vance paused and looked over at Marcy and then down at Robbie. "The thing I want all three of you to remember is that he's still your father. No matter what he looks like or sounds like or what he can do or can't do. He's still your dad, no matter what."

Another lake of silence spread across the minutes.

"And I also want you to remember," Dr. Vance finally said, "that you always need to talk about your feelings, okay? There are no bad feelings. There are no right feelings or wrong feelings. You feel what you feel."

Marcy said, "So we should come and talk to you?"

Dr. Vance smiled. "Well, sweetie, no. This is what's called an 'initial consultation.' Somebody else will be assigned to your family for ongoing visits. And you can talk to your mother, or your friends, or a teacher, whenever you need to, okay?"

She reached into her briefcase, a slab of shiny black leather that she'd perched on the floor next to her shoes, so that she never lost physical contact with it. She fished out four small white rectangles of paper.

Among the bits of information on the paper was this:

Gloria P. Vance
M.S.W., Ph.D.

She handed a card to me, then she gave one to Marcy, one to Robbie, and one to Mom.

We all held on to our little cards and looked at her.

Dr. Vance said, "Are there any questions for right now? Anything at all?"

Mom still held Robbie in her arms and was rocking back and forth with him. It almost seemed like she ought to be singing when she did that, singing a lullaby, but of course she wasn't singing. This was not the time to be singing.

"Dr. Vance," Mom said. She started out talking slowly, but her voice got faster. And stronger. "Let me ask you something. From the first minute all of this started, from the very first, I've tried to get some information about what happened to my husband.

About the accident, I mean. But I can't get any details. And I'd really like to know."

"Well, Mrs. Browning, you see—"

"No. Hold on." Mom's voice was sharp. "I keep getting the runaround. Everywhere I turn. Even when I was at Walter Reed, even with all of those military people right there, I got, like, zilch. Nothing. Nobody would tell me a damned thing."

We were completely shocked. We'd never heard our mother say a curse word before. We were in a strange new place now. Where anything could happen.

My fingers tingled, just from the sudden surprise of it. It wasn't a bad feeling. It was kind of exciting.

"Mrs. Browning," Dr. Vance said calmly, "as I've tried to explain—"

"No, no, no, no, *no*," Mom said, shaking her head as she interrupted Dr. Vance. "You haven't explained anything at all." The fact that she'd interrupted somebody was another wild shock. Now my ears were sort of tingling, too, because I realized it was true: anything *could* happen now. Anything.

My mother was sitting on the floor with Robbie, so she had to look up at Dr. Vance. You'd think that would give Dr. Vance the upper hand, that it would automatically make Dr. Vance the boss. But, no: Mom was in charge, just for the moment. Her anger and her fierceness and the curse word and the interrupting— obviously, she was totally in charge. It was great.

"And we want to know what happened," Mom said. "That's all. What happened to him? How did it happen? We know Ed was in a truck, an armored vehicle, and that he got hit. But that's all we know."

Dr. Vance gave my mother a look that I'd seen grown-ups give each other plenty of times. What it meant was: *Is this what you want? Do you really want to do this now? Do you?*

"The army," Mom went on, as if she didn't even notice the look, "won't tell us a damned thing. I keep calling my senator. Somebody from her office always calls me back, but it doesn't matter. Nobody answers my questions. There's nothing. Not a peep. Not a bit of information. I know that other people were wounded, too, in the convoy that day. And I know that somebody died. But I'd like to know where that truck was going, and why. I'd just like to know what the mission was. The job. The assignment. The one that left my husband with his leg gone. And his arm. And where it happened. And why the hell they were even there that day. In that spot. And what it meant. And what the mission was *for*, exactly."

I was watching Dr. Vance. She looked as if she'd heard this kind of thing before. Lots of times. She wasn't rattled at all. She wasn't the least bit nervous.

"I'll check into it, Mrs. Browning," she said. "I certainly will."

"We don't know what happened," Mom went on, as if Dr. Vance had never spoken. "We have no idea. We want to know where he was and where it happened. And how they all got there."

My mother was holding Robbie and rocking back and forth, back and forth. Any other time, I might've been embarrassed. I might've wished she'd just stop that. And stop talking, for sure.

But not this time. I kind of wished she'd go on that way forever, holding Robbie, rocking back and forth, while she asked her questions. She asked about why Dad couldn't have stayed longer at Walter Reed, where he'd been making a lot of good progress. She asked about why there wasn't a special hospital in town for people with brain injuries. She asked why there wasn't more information available about people with brain injuries—not just for us, the families involved, but for the rest of the country, so they'd understand. Didn't anybody care? Didn't anybody see what these men and women had given up? How their lives were changed forever? And the lives of their families, their children? How things would never, ever be the same again?

She looked right at Dr. Vance and she kept asking. Asking and asking and asking.

And Dr. Vance answered.

But not really. Her answers reminded me of the kind of answers you try to get by with in school, when the teacher calls on you and you haven't read the assignment but you don't want to admit it. So you let your words kind of slide around inside the sentence, as if it's all just way too complicated.

Dr. Vance's answers were a little bit better than that, but not much. The weirdest part of it all was that she never got mad at Mom's questions, which were getting sharper and sharper. Dr. Vance was calm. The madder Mom got, the calmer Dr. Vance was. It was strange. But you couldn't hate Dr. Vance. She was trying. You could tell she was trying.

That's what seemed to really get to my mother: everybody was polite, and everybody was trying. Everybody was doing their best. It could drive you crazy.

And then he started to talk.

Just like that, Dad started talking again. Not just grunts and groans. Words. Short sentences, sometimes, but mostly just words. We could figure out what he wanted. We didn't have to guess anymore.

"TV," he'd say. "I want some TV." He meant he wanted to watch TV, but he said it like he wanted more mashed potatoes or something. It was funny to hear it that way.

Sometimes he used the wrong word. He'd say, "Chair," when what he wanted was a pillow. Or he'd say, "Fan," and he wanted something to drink. It was weird. But you got used to it. It wasn't so bad. You had to watch where he pointed with his good arm, or watch his eyes, and then you could figure out what he really wanted, no matter what he said.

Dad still wouldn't walk much. He was supposed to practice getting up and walking a few steps, every day, like they'd taught him to do in the hospital, but he wouldn't do it. He just wouldn't.

I heard Mom on the phone once. I'm not sure who she was talking to, but I heard her say, "Well, I can't force him, can I? I can't *force* him to get up."

I could sort of understand why Dad didn't want to get up and walk. It was very hard. I mean, it was hard just watching him try. It would have been a whole lot harder to be the one who actually had to do the trying.

He'd have to lift himself out of the wheelchair with his good arm and then stand up.

It was jerky and slow. It looked like a robot. He didn't have good balance on his prosthetic leg—I knew the words pretty well by now—and he looked like somebody who was drunk or maybe really clumsy.

He'd put a leg out and then just stand there for a long time, like he'd forgotten how to take the next step.

Then he'd twist his hips and move the other leg out and wait again for the same long time. You wondered, while he waited and you waited, too, if he was going to fall over sometime. If his balance would fly away from him, just like that.

Another step.

Then he waited.

Another step.

That was usually about it. Dad never took more than two or three steps. Then he'd wave toward his wheelchair, to tell us he wanted us to bring it to him. He'd fall back down in it.

At first, when you watched him try to walk, the few times he tried it, you remembered what he was like before. Dad liked to go fishing with his brothers, and he liked to play basketball with Marcy in the driveway. Sometimes he'd pick up Robbie and put him over his shoulder and march through the house, pretending Robbie was a sack of potatoes—*I've got some potatoes here, anybody want a sack of fresh potatoes?*— and Robbie would giggle and squeal.

If you watched Dad now, you had to remember those times. And then, after a while, you didn't remember them so much anymore, or at least not so clearly.

It was all like a dream, and it didn't matter. When you thought about Dad now, you thought about the wheelchair. The rest of it was gone. Mostly.

Everything had changed.

Nothing had changed.

We still went to school. We got up in the morning and had Pop-Tarts or a bowl of Raisin Bran or Lucky Charms, and then we got on the bus and went to school. We came home and we played.

The difference was, Dad was there. All the time. He never left.

Where could he go? How could he get there?

Before, he'd be at work a lot of the time. Now, he never left the house. He was always there.

Another difference was that other people were around a lot more. The physical therapist, the counselor, some people from the army who had papers for Dad to sign. Somebody from an insurance company and then somebody from Consolidated Power. Talking about something called "long-term disability." Long-term. Long-term. When you said it, when you heard it, it sounded like it had an echo built right into it: *long-term*.

There was family around, too. A lot of people from my mom's and dad's family. At first.

Later, not so many.

In July, we found out what had happened to Dad in Iraq.

It was just an ordinary thing in Iraq. It happens, they told us, every day. Day after day.

Dad and his outfit were in a line of Humvees. They were helping a bunch of trucks take supplies to one of the places where the American soldiers live in Iraq.

There was an attack on the line of trucks and Humvees. The one Dad was riding in was hurt the worst. It was on fire, we heard, and they had to pull the soldiers out.

Dad wasn't injured in the fire, though. He was one of the first soldiers they got out of the Humvee. His leg had gotten all torn up the blast, and his arm, too, but he wasn't on fire.

The person who told us most of this was named Nelson Guthridge. He was in my father's National Guard unit. Nelson Guthridge didn't go to Iraq. He stayed back here. But he knew what happened to Dad and the other people, and he told Mom in July.

I don't know why he waited so long to give us the details. He never really explained that. Maybe he didn't know for a while, either.

Nelson Guthridge came by our house on a Tuesday afternoon, when the physical therapist was working with Dad on the back patio. You could hear the physical therapist, whose name was Stacy, talking to Dad in her cheerful voice: "Okay, Mr. Browning! Up we go! Okay, handsome! Let's get going!"

In the kitchen, Mom was sitting at the table with Nelson Guthridge. She had set out a pitcher of iced tea. There were ice cubes bobbing across the light brown surface of the tea and a lemon slice that rode in the middle like a little yellow raft.

Mom poured a glass for Nelson Guthridge and a glass for herself.

Marcy and I were sitting at the table, too. Robbie sat on Mom's lap. He played with her bracelet while she talked to Nelson Guthridge.

Mom didn't ask us to leave and give her and Nelson Guthridge some privacy. That was not how our family operated now. There was no such thing as privacy.

We weren't separate people anymore. We were all piled together. We didn't see ourselves as kids and adults, as Denise and Ed Browning and their kids Rachel, Marcy, and Robbie.

We were all one thing now. This blur. Our family didn't have the normal lines or spaces anymore. One person flowed right into the next person, and the next and the next. I guess it sounds like kind of a mess, but it didn't feel that way. It was the way we had to be, so that we could live. There wasn't time to worry about each little piece of our family anymore. We had to be one big thing that did the best it could, every day.

So we were sitting there when Nelson Guthridge told Mom about what happened to Dad in Iraq. About the Humvee. And the fire.

About Dad's leg and his arm.

About his friend Sam, who died.

About Amy, who didn't. "But probably wishes she did," Nelson Guthridge said, shaking his head. He had greasy, raggedy hair that looked like the mop that Mom kept on the back patio, just before she threw it away, and a sad face.

He talked like that right in front of us. Grim talk. Grown-up talk, filled with things he knew about the world that we didn't know. Nelson Guthridge's talk seemed to have nails driven into it. Nails that you'd come across when you sorted through it later, trying to remember what he'd said, and you'd be hurt before you knew what hit you.

Nelson Guthridge drank his tea and then licked his brown lips and said, "She's pretty bad off, let me tell you. Amy Weatherall. Two little kids. Husband's out of the picture. And she's a quadraplegic. Lotsa scars, from the fire. They can't do nothing for her." He held up his glass and waggled it, which seemed to be his way of telling Mom he wanted more.

She poured. He pulled his glass back and nearly emptied it a second time before he spoke again.

"Anyways," Nelson Guthridge said, "it was just a regular old patrol. Routine. There ain't no cover-up or nothing, which is why I came by to talk to you. I figured, since the army never tells nobody nothing, that you might think otherwise. You might be thinking there's some big story here, that the army's got something to hide, but that ain't it. It's just a regular old army screwup, I'm telling you. Wrong place, wrong time. Them big old Humvees and then them little Iraqis running around, taking potshots. Kids and old ladies, sometimes, so you don't even know who to look out for. And listen."

Nelson Guthridge turned his glass around in a circle, as if he were hunting for another edge of the rim to sip from, but I could tell it was just something he did when he was nervous. "I'll say this, Mrs. Browning. Eddie's a hell of a lot better off than Amy Weatherall. A *hell* of a lot."

When Nelson Guthridge had come in the door that afternoon, Dad didn't recognize him. Dad didn't react at all. He just sat there in his wheelchair, head sunk down. A lot of Dad's hair had grown back by then, so you couldn't see that weird purple line anymore.

Nelson Guthridge didn't seem to mind that Dad didn't know him. He just went right up to Dad and said, "Hey, Eddie. How's it going?"

Dad got kind of excited then, which is what he did sometimes when new things happened. He'd get all riled up. It was like he wasn't in charge of himself anymore.

Dad was rocking in his wheelchair, and pounding on the armrest with his good hand. "Hey, hey, hey, hey," he said, in a rush. After Nelson Guthridge said, "Hey, bro," Dad kept saying, "Hey, bro. Hey, bro."

Nelson Guthridge laughed. You might think it was a nice kind of laugh, that he was laughing with Dad and they were sharing something, but it didn't seem that way to me. It seemed to me that Nelson Guthridge thought it was kind of funny. Seeing Dad like that. Strange and funny. But I couldn't say anything to anybody about that. About what it felt like to me.

"Hey, bro," Nelson Guthridge said back to Dad.

"Hey, bro!" Dad said.

And then Dad's physical therapist came. They had to start the session, so Mom and Nelson Guthridge and the rest of us—like I said, we moved as a group without thinking much about it—went into the kitchen. And Nelson Guthridge told us about what happened to Dad in Iraq.

"Everybody wants this big story. Everybody wants, like, some kind of movie," Nelson Guthridge said. "They want there to be some kind of cover-up. Like it was maybe CIA or a spy thing going on. They want it to be some kind of secret mission or something." Nelson Guthridge shook his big greasy head, as if he'd wised up a long time ago but he knew you had to let the suckers believe what they wanted to believe. That's what made them suckers. "Wasn't nothing like that," he went on. "It was just a regular old attack by a bunch of diaper-heads who don't know nothing about Jesus—and if you ask me, we can't send 'em to hell fast enough."

Somebody nodded. It could have been Marcy, or Robbie, or Mom, or me. Like I said, it was like we'd become one large blob, a single organism, and it was hard sometimes to tell where one person left off and another one began. Our bodies didn't stop at our skins anymore. Everything ran together.

Somebody nodded, and in the seconds before Nelson Guthridge spoke again, you could hear Stacy's voice from out on the back patio with Dad. She was fiercely cheerful: "Come on, Mr. Browning! You've got to try! It's all up to you, Mr. Browning!"

And then Nelson Guthridge was speaking again. He didn't seem to be paying much attention to what was going on out on the patio. He was focused on his iced-tea glass, which he held tightly between two wide palms, held for a long time, almost as if a part of him wanted to crush that glass. Just smash it, for no special reason.

"A regular old screwup," he said. "That's the army for you. That's the good old U.S.A. Listen, your daddy and all the rest of 'em didn't have a chance. Sitting ducks. No chance at all. I'm telling you. Just a big screwup."

7. RAMP

Uncle Steve and Uncle Travis and our neighbor Frank Weber were working on our house.

There was a lot of stuff that had to be done. Dad needed a ramp to get from the driveway to the front door. He also needed to have the doors to a lot of rooms made wider: bathroom, kitchen. The way they were now, he couldn't get the wheelchair through them. Or if he could get it through, it was a tight fit. And Mom said that even when he was able to walk just fine with his new leg, a day that was "just around the corner," he'd still need to use the wheelchair sometimes. When he got tired.

Also, there were things they needed to do to the bathroom, so Dad could use it on his own. They'd need to put in lots of handlebars. Things he could grab with his good hand. They had to raise the toilet seat. And lower the countertop.

They started the job at about five on a Saturday morning in August. Everybody showed up at once: Uncle Travis, Uncle Steve, and Frank Weber. They were coming from different places, but they got there at almost the same time, which made Mom laugh.

"Hi, guys!" she said. "We've got coffee. *Lots* of it."

She had come out on the front porch when she heard the sound of Frank Weber's truck in our driveway. He had a big silver truck with a ladder rack in back and, also in the back, a huge black toolbox that looked like a pirate's treasure chest. Even though he lived close, Frank Weber had driven over because he needed to bring his tools: hammers and saws and crowbars and chisels and nail guns and cordless drills.

Just as Frank Weber was sliding out of his truck, here came Steve and Travis in Steve's black Chevy Blazer. They had been on the road for about three hours that morning. When they got out of the SUV—I was standing right behind Mom on the front porch—they looked sort of like ghosts, because it was so early to be seeing them, and the sky was still pretty dark, and for just a minute or two it seemed more like a dream than like real life.

They looked a little tired already, before they even got started. Their T-shirts were all wrinkled. Their shorts drooped in the rear end.

I knew Steve and Travis pretty well, but only in certain ways: I knew them as uncles, as relatives. Not as working men who showed up to do a job. I knew them as jokers who would tease you about things: your haircut, your new glasses, the boyfriend you didn't have.

But today, they weren't jokers. They were serious men with a lot of things they had to get done, and they brushed right past me and Marcy and Robbie like we were just something else in their way. To Mom, Travis said, "Better keep the kids out of here, Den," and he said it in a dark, blank voice. A stranger's voice. It was shocking to me. We were just things they had to work around. Extra problems.

They seemed to be in a bad mood. And there was nothing we could do about it. Only Frank Weber was normal and friendly.

Mom gave them coffee. She had the mugs all

ready on the kitchen counter, lined up in a neat row, with all of the handles facing in the same direction. She'd made cinnamon rolls, too. Frank Weber ate two but Steve and Travis didn't take any.

Before they got started, they stood in the kitchen drinking coffee, three men and our mother. Nobody sat down. It wasn't a day for sitting down. They held their coffee mugs with both hands while they leaned against the kitchen counter, and they drank the coffee in a few long swallows. Then they'd wince, because the coffee was pretty hot. But they never learned from their mistake: they'd take another big drink and wince again.

Frank Weber finished each cinnamon roll in exactly two bites. He swiped a thumb against the sides of his mouth, to capture any of the flaked sugar glaze that might still be there, and then he'd pop the thumb in his mouth to suck off the sweetness.

"Beats a napkin any day," Frank Weber said, grinning.

When Mom had offered him a second cinnamon roll, he'd shrugged his big shrug and said, "Sure, why not?"

They were discussing what they were going to do

that day. They knew they couldn't finish everything. There was just too much. But the order of things was important.

Uncle Travis seemed to know more than the other two did. They'd start talking about ripping off trim board and punching through drywall, and Travis would shake his head in an irritated way and say, "Guys, listen, you can't do it like that," and then he'd outline a plan. He moved his hands in the air to make shapes and show distances.

Travis and Steve: Dad's brothers.

Travis is tall, with dark bushy hair that he usually squashes under a red baseball cap. Steve's hair is flat and brown. It always looks kind of greasy to me. Steve is skinnier than Travis.

If you saw the three of them lined up, Dad and Travis and Steve, you'd know they were brothers. Their faces have the same shape, even though their eyes are different colors and their hair isn't the same and Steve has a scraggly beard. Side by side, they look like funny little echoes of each other.

But if you saw them separately, you might not believe they were brothers at all.

I think it's the same way with me and Marcy and Rob. Sometimes we look like we're just broken-off pieces of the same basic thing. Pretty much alike. Other times, though, when we're not standing in a row, we don't look like we're even related. You have to know. If you just looked at us, you wouldn't be able to figure it out. Somebody would have to tell you.

Dad sat in his wheelchair, watching.

He watched his brothers and Frank Weber work.

He still didn't talk much, but he was paying better attention to things now. He didn't keep his head down all the time. He'd actually look at you.

Which was both good and bad.

They did the ramp first.

They couldn't finish everything that weekend—in fact, it would take them five more weekends through the fall to get it all done—but they got a good start on the ramp.

Frank Weber had built ramps before. He had built

them for government office buildings. Once for a school. I heard him telling Mom about it. Still, Travis was in charge. You could just tell. Frank Weber would measure and then measure again, and put these little wooden stakes in the ground and tie a string from one stake to the next, but Travis was the boss: it was Travis who said, "Okay, let's do it," and then Steve would dig holes for the posts with a tool that Frank told me was called—*duh*—a post-hole digger, and then Frank would mix the cement in the wheelbarrow. The cement was going to go in those little holes. Frank told me that, too. Then the posts would be centered in the cement. That would make them straight and stable. Something you could count on.

If you asked Travis what was going on, he'd frown and kind of wave his hand like there was a fly in his face, which was his way of telling you to go away without actually saying it out loud. Frank Weber, though, liked to explain things. He'd give you the reasons why they were doing what they were doing, and then tell you how it all fit together.

Our house was changing. A lot. I didn't like it, but I didn't say anything about it.

Everything was changing.

First Dad changed, and then all the other changes had to come because he changed.

I was mad about it, even though I didn't know exactly what to be mad at: at all the changes, or at Dad, or at the world in general.

I couldn't be mad at my father. That wouldn't be right. He hadn't done anything to cause all of this. Things had just happened. All these terrible things.

Everything was different now, and there was nobody to blame. So the anger had nowhere to go, no direction, no escape. There were times when I looked at him and I just wanted to start yelling at him. I wanted him to fight back. I wanted him to try to be who he'd been before. But he just sat there, day after day. I had learned enough about brain injury now to get it: "fighting back" was something your brain had to do, and if you brain couldn't do it, it didn't happen. You could lose your arm and your leg and still fight back. You could be in a wheelchair and still fight back. But your brain was different.

I understood all of that, but I still got mad. I still wanted to yell at him sometimes, which was totally unfair. I knew that. But fair or not, that's how I felt.

That night, a long time after Uncle Steve and Uncle Travis and Frank Weber packed the tools back in Frank Weber's truck and cleaned up the mess they'd made, after Steve and Travis had told Mom no, they'd rather just stay in a motel and get back there first thing Sunday morning, after Frank Weber had asked Mom if we'd like to come over for dinner because Jessica said it would be a good idea and Mom said, "No, thank you, we're all pretty tired"—after all that, I heard Mom on the phone.

It was very, very late. I was still awake, but it was so late that I didn't think anybody else in the world could possibly be awake, too.

I got out of my bed and headed to the kitchen for a glass of water. I didn't have to worry about being quiet for Dad. They gave Dad pills to help him sleep, and those pills really did their job. The problem wasn't keeping Dad asleep. The problem was getting him to wake up.

I stopped in the doorway of the kitchen. The kitchen was dark. I was still in the shadow of the hallway, so Mom couldn't see me.

She sat at the table, looking down, holding the cordless phone to her ear. The palm of her other hand was pressed against her forehead, pushing tight, as if she were trying to keep her thoughts from spilling out.

She was talking softly, so softly that I could barely hear her. I leaned forward, though, from my place in the shadows, because I wanted to hear her.

I leaned. I listened.

I don't know who she was talking to, or who'd called who, or if this was the first time she'd said these things, or the fiftieth time.

I don't know any of that. I won't ever know— because I can't ask her, because I wasn't supposed to be listening. I won't ever know if this was the only time she'd had these feelings or if they stayed with her all the time, if maybe they ran around her brain like a bunch of ants you find under a rock and no matter how many of them you stomp on, there will always be more and more and more, and they all look exactly alike, which somehow makes it worse. I would never know.

"I think I'm going crazy," she was saying into the phone. Her voice was soft, but it was hard, too. Her voice came out in soft hisses. "Really, I just can't—" She talked in short, chopped-off sentences. "I can't stand it sometimes. I mean, I just—" Maybe if she divided up her sentences into smaller ones, the things she was saying wouldn't sound so bad. Maybe that's what she thought. "I just—I just *hate* all this. I hate, hate, hate, hate, *hate* it. I hate it all the time. It's not—"

She was crying now—not big, husky sobs but a kind of soft, whimpering crying that sounded a little bit like rain you can barely hear sometimes, rain that's way in the distance—and then she said, "It's like—it's like there's nothing left anymore. You know? Like he's—he's—he's just *sitting* there. He sits there all day—he just *sits there*, and there's really *nothing there*. And—it's like he's just this body with nothing attached to it anymore. Like he's—he's a *back*. Just a back. That's all he's got now. His back. This thing. He's got this thing in the center of him, this core, this thing that keeps his whole body from just falling in on itself, but that's all. That's it. A back. A *back*. A—"

The crying broke off, and then Mom took a bunch of deep breaths. In and out, in and out, like she was following instructions from the person on the other end of that phone, without thinking too much about it. Just doing whatever the person told her to do, to get through the next two minutes of her life, and then the next two minutes after that.

"Yeah," Mom said, after all the breaths. "Yeah, that's it, exactly. That's the thing. That's—" She laughed, but it wasn't a happy laugh. It was a laugh I didn't like at all. It had an edge to it, something crisp and bitter. "I'm awful, right? I'm a terrible person. I'm a monster. I'm going to hell. Straight to hell." Another laugh, another bad, scary laugh. "But it couldn't be worse," she said. "Could it? Could it, really? I mean, hell really couldn't be a whole lot worse than what we're going through right now. You know?"

They'd met in college, my mother and father. A lot of parents had met in college, I found out. It was a normal way to meet.

Dad was a political-science major. He explained it all to me when I was in third grade. We sat down one night after dinner, just the two of us, and he told me the whole story.

His original plan, he said, was to go to law school after he finished college. His father—my grandfather, Edward Jerome Browning—had been a lawyer. But he'd died before Dad and Mom even met each other.

He met Mom at a party, Dad said. They were both at the same college party. She wanted to be a history teacher someday.

They liked each other right away, Dad said, and then they got married.

He didn't go to law school, after all. I asked him why not, and he made a funny face like he was thinking hard about it—he bunched up his chin, frowned, and rolled his eyes toward the ceiling—and then he leaned forward suddenly and poked me in the belly with his finger and said, "You! *You're* the reason!"

I giggled, and Dad went on. "You see, Rachel,

your mom and I found out that you were on the way, and we were *so* happy that we decided I wouldn't go to law school. I'd get a job and we'd get ready to say hello to *you*—to Rachel Ann Browning!"

He poked me in the belly again. I giggled again. I couldn't help it. It tickled.

"And then," Dad said, "we found out about Marcy coming."

"And then Robbie," I said.

"Yep, and then Robbie," he agreed, with a big happy nod.

Mom, he told me, had decided not to be a history teacher, either. Maybe she'd be a history teacher later, after we were all grown up.

"I went to work for ConPow, and now I make sure people have electricity so they can watch TV and wash their clothes and everything else," Dad said. "Just think. If we didn't have electricity, we couldn't run our computers or cook dinner or stay warm in the wintertime."

It's kind of embarrassing to admit now, but I didn't know anything about electricity then. It might as well have been some kind of magic. I mean, you reached up and you flipped the switch and the lights went on: that's all I knew. I liked the word *electricity* but I couldn't picture it in my head. I could only see the results of it, only what it actually *did*.

And I knew that when it didn't work right, Dad had to go to the office so he could explain to people what had happened and when they could expect to have their electricity up and running again.

When I was in fourth grade, Mom got her real-estate license and started selling houses part-time. I remember that the *real* in *real estate* was another tricky word for me at the time, like *electricity*, but I didn't want to ask too many questions. There are some things you just have to figure out on your own.

You can see photos of my mom and dad. There are a lot of photos. Dad is tall and has brown hair that flops over on his forehead, and he has these ears that sort of stick out. Robbie has the same kind of ears, and when you see them together, Dad and Robbie, it almost looks like they're having a contest to see whose ears can grow the biggest.

Mom, in most of the pictures, looks shy and embarrassed. She's usually glancing down at the ground or off to the side. She's smiling, but it's a smile that looks like somebody just said, "Hey, let's have a smile!" It's not like she wanted to smile, or even would've thought of smiling, if somebody hadn't asked her to.

In the pictures we have of Mom and Dad, Mom is a lot shorter than Dad. He puts an arm around her shoulder. She hooks an arm around his waist. They're always touching each other.

Right after I asked Dad about how he and Mom met, I asked Mom why she and Dad got married. It seemed like such a weird thing, to meet a stranger at a party and then spend your whole life with them.

"Well, sweetie," she said, "that's just how it is. There's a time in your life when you leave your old family—your mother and father—and you go off and make a new family. A different one. And that's your family forever after."

That wasn't the answer I was looking for. I'd hoped she would talk about love and stuff, and about "falling in love" with Dad and about him "falling in love" with her. All of that. All of the stuff that, when I thought about it, made me feel sort of squishy inside but that also scared me, just a little bit.

But she didn't. She talked about families and children and jobs. About deciding where you wanted your new life to be and buying a house there and "putting down roots."

It was kind of disappointing, really. Because I was expecting a completely different kind of story. A soft and mushy one. I wanted to know how you could look at somebody and then say, *Okay, that's it. Here it is: the rest of my life.*

Instead Mom told me another story, a story about houses and careers and what she kept calling "responsibility"—another word that, like *electricity*, is hard to comprehend. It's too abstract. You only know it's there by looking at the results of what it does.

It wasn't the story I wanted to hear, but it was still a good story.

They finished the ramp on Sunday night. Then Uncle Travis and Uncle Steve drove away. They seemed very tired, and they seemed to be mad about something, too, although they didn't seem to be mad at any of us. It just hung in the air, their anger.

Before he left that night, Frank Weber pounded the rail on that ramp with his big fist and he said, "Looks like that'll hold up, don't you think?" and he grinned. Then he went home, too.

They'd be back soon to do the rest: the doorways, the bathroom.

There was still lots and lots to do.

A couple of days later, Robbie came home crying. He'd been playing over at Jeff's, and another kid was there, too, and the other kid said Robbie's dad was a vegetable.

Robbie told the story right in front of Dad, right there in the living room. I thought Mom might try to get him to stop, to not talk about it, because it might hurt Dad's feelings.

But she didn't. She let Robbie go through his story, and then she hugged him. She said, "Well, Robbie, honey, some people are just naturally mean.

I'm glad you came home. You don't have to play with that little boy anymore." And then she said, "That's a nasty thing for somebody to say. Your daddy isn't a vegetable. Nobody is. It's a horrible thing to say."

I was standing there when Robbie told the story, and I wondered how Dad felt about it. People were always talking about him. Outside the house, inside the house. They talked about him. Wouldn't that make you a little bit mad? Wouldn't you want to jump up and say, *Stop it, leave us all alone?*

But Dad just sat there. I was still learning about all that the brain does. Just when I thought I understood it, something else would happen and I'd realize how much more I still had to learn. It turns out that part of what your brain does for you—a huge, important part—is to get you to do things. It's not just knowing *how* to do things, like drive a car or tie your shoes or get out of bed in the morning or fight back when you're mad. It's the *push* to do those things. The will. A word I heard a lot from the therapists was *initiative*. Your brain gives you initiative. And one of the parts of Dad's brain that had been hurt was the part with the initiative.

So Dad just sat there, with his fake leg and his fake arm.

I'd stopped saying "artificial." Now I just said "fake." It was easier. And I didn't bother with "prosthesis" anymore, either.

I couldn't tell if Robbie knew what "vegetable" meant in relation to a person, but he knew it wasn't good.

With little kids, it's not about the words. It's about how the words are said. You know it's a bad word, a word that's meant to hurt you, by the look on the face of the kid who's saying it to you. Not by the word itself.

The word is nothing. The word's just a way to get the meanness across.

By October, Dad was going to a rehab center four times a week.

A van came to pick him up in the morning, even before Marcy and Robbie and I left for school. He'd be gone until dinnertime. Then the van would pull into our driveway, and the driver would get out and come around to the other side.

The side door would open, and a black metal platform would slide out of the van. Dad's wheelchair was hooked to the platform. It moved kind of jerky and rough, and I always wondered if it was scary to Dad, riding on that platform, being hauled out of the van.

When the platform got to the ground, the driver waited. Dad was supposed to stand up and walk. He wasn't supposed to use the wheelchair all the time. He was supposed to walk like a normal person.

But he wouldn't do it. And the driver couldn't make him, I guess. "Nobody can make him," Mom had said one day, while we watched from the picture window in the living room. "Nobody can really make you do anything. Not if you don't want to do it."

The tone of her voice surprised me. It was hard and kind of mean. Not as mean, probably, as the kid who teased Robbie, but still mean. It didn't have any of the things in it that somebody Robbie's age expects to hear in a mother's voice, those soft warm things that actually are the reason you ask her lots of questions, even dumb questions you already know the answers to: you want to hear those things in her voice. So you keep her talking.

But this voice was cold. We watched the van driver just stand in our driveway in front of Dad's wheelchair, and we watched Dad sit there. He wouldn't get up on his fake leg, the way he was supposed to, and he wouldn't even push himself up the ramp in the wheelchair. He was waiting for somebody to do it all for him. "Which, in the long run, doesn't help him at all, not really," Mom had told us.

In her cold voice, Mom said, "He'd probably just sit there all night long, if nobody forced him." She shook her head. "He won't do a thing. He won't even try." Like me, she didn't understand about initiative. She thought she understood, maybe, but she really didn't. Or maybe understanding was a thing that could come and go.

For months she had been so calm with Dad. So patient. So nice, all the time. She'd tell him to take it slow and be careful, to do what he could. She'd tell him we loved him and we all knew he was going through a rough time, and nobody expected him to be perfect or to always have loads of energy. He should pace himself. He should do his best and that was fine. That would always be just fine.

But here she was, on the night before Halloween, when the air was starting to get sharper and the sky was getting darker a little bit earlier every day, and she looked out the living room window at Dad and she sounded a little bit mean. Not mad, but mean. Or maybe it was just disappointment, a disappointment so intense that it was like a fist closing around her heart.

Just what *is* a body, anyway? Your legs and arms? Your head?

All of it, of course.

But what if part of your body is gone? How much could you take away, how many pieces, and have it still be *you*?

There were times when he didn't seem to be my dad at all. And then there were times when he seemed more like my dad than ever before—almost as if, when they stripped away pieces of him, they'd taken away the things that really didn't matter, anyway, and left only the part of him that did matter. And that part could grow stronger. Without all those other parts around to distract you, maybe you could see the real person.

That was how I thought about it sometimes. I realize it's a pretty strange thing to think. But you could spend your life searching for what makes you "you"—this unique, distinctive person—and my father had just gotten a big head start on that process. Some of the other parts had been taken away and here he was: himself. I would look at him sometimes, just sitting there, and I'd start to think about what makes us who we are. The things that happen to us? Our families? Or is there something else, some core that doesn't change?

Sometimes I really thought my dad was still my dad, just quieter and slower. Different, sure, but maybe that was okay. Most of the time, though, I just felt sad.

I don't know what Dad felt. These days, he didn't tell us how he felt.

Mom said it was because he didn't have the right words anymore. The only words he had left were for things—TV, a spoon, a drink of water—and not for feelings.

Feelings, I guess, you can live without. But you have to have things.

Just after Thanksgiving, I went out to the backyard and tore down the fort.

I kicked at the sticks that held up the walls, which made the plywood roof collapse, and then I grabbed the plywood sheet with both hands and tried to throw it against the tree. It was too heavy. It just flopped over. The whole thing was a mess now, which satisfied me.

Don't ask me why I did it, because I can't tell you.

Okay, maybe I really did know. Maybe it was this: the fort was part of my old life, the one we didn't have anymore. I was just sick of looking at it. Every day, there it was in the backyard, almost as if it was waiting for us to come back to what we'd been before. But we couldn't. There was no way we could get there. It was too far away.

So I had to destroy the fort. I didn't want to look at it anymore. I didn't want to think about it being out there. Waiting. So it had to go.

☩

I told Dad what I'd done. I told him right away, because I didn't want him to see it and wonder what had happened. I didn't want him to think a hard rain had done it, or that some kid in the neighborhood had sneaked over and attacked it. I wanted him to know that it was my decision.

He looked at me.

We were sitting in the living room, just before dinner on the day I did it. The day I'd smashed up the fort. His wheelchair was parked in front of the TV set. Dad had to turn his head sideways to look at me on the couch.

He made a noise. I guess he wanted to let me know he'd heard what I said.

"Yeah, I tore down the fort," I repeated. "It was stupid. I'm way too old to have a fort."

Dad and I didn't have a lot of conversations these days. Not when it was just the two of us. Usually, there were other people around. But this time, it was just us.

"Why?" he said.

"I told you. It was stupid."

"Stupid."

"Yeah." I hated it when he repeated words back to me like that, which he did a lot. It was like he was trying the word out, testing it, making sure the meaning was still inside it, making sure it hadn't leaked away when he wasn't looking.

"Stupid?" he said.

"Yeah, that's what I said—*stupid*. Stupid, stupid, stupid." I was sounding mean now, but I couldn't stop myself. "It doesn't matter, okay? It was just a stupid fort. It doesn't matter. Nobody cares. I never really liked it, anyway. I just said I did. I just said it to make everybody feel better. But I didn't."

It was one of the few times after Dad came back that I was mean to him on purpose. I didn't want to be mean, but I was. And it wasn't because of anything he had done or hadn't done. Right then, I just wanted to wipe out everything that was in front of me, or at least the things I could get my hands on. I wanted to leave a trail of busted-up things. I hated the wheelchair. I hated the space it took up in the living room, the way it blocked things. I hated it when Dad repeated words back to me. I hated how slow he was. I hated how Mom talked to him—in big, soft, round words, careful words, except for the times when she'd lose her temper and then her words would be pointed, broken-off, and it was like she was using them to jab and pierce. I hated my friends. They wouldn't talk much about Dad. If they did talk about him, they said nice, hopeful things. Useless things. But most of all, I hated that fort. It had to go.

And then at some point, while I was still sitting there in the living room with Dad that night, I didn't hate anything anymore. It went away, all that hatred. It just drained away. I was back. I was me again: Brownie. The girl who used to love *A Wrinkle in Time*. The girl who loves pizza and green socks and Batman movies. And Dad.

Just like that, I went from being this mean person, with all these terrible thoughts, back to being who I really was. I settled down. I didn't hug him or touch him—that would have been way too weird— but I smiled at him, and Dad smiled back. I think he was probably just repeating what he saw, just like he would repeat what he heard, but I didn't care.

From then on, I started going back and forth.

Bouncing between anger and peace. Between mean-ness and stillness. These little storms would take hold, like somebody grabbing my shoulder and shaking me, and I couldn't break free. And then I did break free. The storms never lasted very long, but they did happen. I got pretty good at hiding my moods, so that people wouldn't know about some of the ter-rible thoughts I had, the mean and ugly thoughts. I was ashamed of them, even though they only lasted a little while.

I wanted to ask him things I knew he couldn't answer. Like: Why had he let this happen to him? Why wasn't he more careful? Why hadn't he taken better care of himself? Why did he have to go over there in the first place, just because somebody told him to? Couldn't he have said no? None of my friends' fathers or mothers had gone to Iraq. Why did it have to be *him*?

And I was still glad that I had smashed that fort. Even when I felt better, I was glad the fort was gone. For a while.

Right after I tore down the fort I made a new friend, even though I wasn't looking for a new friend. I met this guy at a family therapy group meeting that we went to.

I didn't want to go. My mom, I could tell, didn't really want to go, either, but I think the whole fort thing got her a little worried about me. Marcy and Robbie were just glad to be going somewhere on a school night, so they were okay with it. But I hated the whole idea.

The hospital sponsored it. One night a month, they'd invite families to come in and talk with other families about their problems. Mom hired a nurse's aide to come and stay with Dad—this was for families, not for the people who'd been injured—and off we went.

There was a big, bright room with orange plastic chairs placed in a circle. There was a table along the back wall, with plates of cookies and one of those coffee urns with the pouring spout that you tip forward and a stack of white Styrofoam cups. For the younger kids, there were juice boxes. I don't much like coffee, but I sure wasn't going to take one of those stupid juice boxes. So I got a cup of coffee, and I picked out a place to sit. I scooted way down in the orange plastic chair, and I stuck my legs straight out in front of me. I wanted anybody who saw me to know that I was already bored.

Robbie grabbed three juice boxes. My mother made him put two of them back. Marcy didn't want anything to drink, but she took a cookie. Then they all sat down, too.

The other families looked like regular people. You couldn't tell, just by looking at them, that they had somebody in their family, too, with a traumatic brain injury.

We were the only ones whose family member had a brain injury from the Iraq war. For everybody else, the injury had come in a normal way: a car accident, a fall, a bike accident. It turns out that there are all kinds of ways that brain injuries can happen. Ways you probably never even thought about. You don't have to be in a war to get hurt really, really bad.

Anyway, the family therapy meeting was not as stupid as I thought it was going to be. I didn't like it, but it wasn't stupid.

We went around the room and said our names and who the family member was, the one who'd gotten hurt. When it was my turn, I said, "Rachel Browning, father," like I was filling out a form. I wanted to keep it simple.

Some of the people, though, went on and on and on, like this was their one big chance to talk about it. "Ruth Lansing," one woman said. She was very fat, and she had gold hoop earrings. "My son Lance is sixteen and he was in a car accident about six months ago. He almost died. He was in a coma for eight days and we didn't think—" She stopped, rooted around in her purse until she found a tissue, then pulled it out and blew her nose with it. She was choked up, but not too choked up to go on. "It's a miracle. That's what it was. A miracle. God wasn't ready to take my baby home."

And then she went off on a long story about the first time he'd opened his eyes after the accident. I have to admit, my mind had started to wander. All I could think about was: *Lance Lansing?* It sounded like somebody in a James Bond movie. It sure didn't sound like a real person.

Marcy was sitting beside me, so after I introduced myself, it was her turn. She said, "Marcia Browning. My daddy was hurt in Iraq." Mom, who was sitting on the other side of Marcy, smiled and put her arm around her and hugged her.

Then it was Mom's turn. She said, "Hello, everyone, I'm Denise Browning. You've already heard from my girls, Rachel and Marcy. In just a minute, you'll meet Robbie." She patted his head. Some of the people, I noticed, looked over at Robbie and grinned. He was paying no attention. He had finished his juice and was now trying to take apart the juice box, picking at the sealed flap on one end of the box and kicking his feet in the air as he did it. The orange plastic chair scooted a bit with each kick. It was annoying, but people don't get mad at little kids for doing things like that.

"We're here," Mom went on, "because my husband, Eddie, was seriously injured in Iraq. In addition to his brain injury, he lost an arm and a leg. He has a long, long road to recovery, but we're very hopeful. He's a fighter."

My mother's words sounded strange to me. This

143

was not the way she usually talked. It sounded as if she was reading off a piece of paper, reading words she'd maybe memorized.

I knew that wasn't true, though. I knew she didn't have any piece of paper. But it still sounded weird and stilted, like somebody giving a report in one of my classes in school.

After we'd gone all the way around the room, the facilitator—that's what she called herself—stood up and said, "That's *great*. Well, it's very encouraging to have all of you here tonight. I know it's not easy. I hope it's the start of a meaningful journey for us all, a journey of sharing and caring." She was about my mother's age, I think. She had long black hair that she wore tied back in a ponytail, and a green sweatshirt with a slogan on it: LIFE IS GOOD. Part of me wondered if she was secretly making fun of us, wearing that particular shirt in front of people like us, but I guess not.

Her name, she told us, was Norma. Then she said that each of us was supposed to find somebody from another family and pair off. Our assignment was to write down all the negative words we'd heard about brain injury. Later, we'd all come back together as a group and talk about how those words made us feel.

And that's how I met Mason. While Norma was handing out sheets of paper and those stubby yellow pencils with no erasers, this guy walked over and stood in front of my chair. He was about my age, I figured. He had frizzy brown hair and ears that stuck out almost as much as Dad's and Robbie's do, which is really saying something.

"Hey," he said. "Mason DeGarmo. Want to be my partner?"

"Okay," I said. I didn't really care. I was just going to write down a few words and then draw pictures on the paper. It seemed like a really dumb exercise.

So Mason dragged our chairs into a corner. I looked over and saw that Marcy had gotten stuck with some old lady. Norma was sitting next to Robbie. *Good luck with that, Norma,* I thought. My mom was paired up with a woman who looked nervous and pale. The woman kept twisting her hands together, the way you do when you're washing your hands. She was incredibly skinny. Her legs looked like sticks.

When I turned back around, Mason was staring

at me, just the way I'd been staring at my mother's partner.

"What?" I said.

"Nothing. I just wondered if you permed your hair."

I hate talking about my hair. It's curly, okay? I can't do anything about that. So lay off. That was the signal I always tried to send when people started talking about it. Actually, I knew why he was asking: guys with curly hair have an even harder time than girls do. So when they see a girl with curly hair, they naturally wonder if she's stuck with it or if she had a choice in the matter. But I didn't know him well enough to start talking about my hair.

"Let's work on the list, okay?" I said. I tried to make my voice very cold.

Mason shrugged. He had pulled his chair right up next to mine. Too close, in fact. So I edged my chair away a little bit.

"Give me a word," he said. He was holding the sheet of paper.

I looked around. The place had that hectic, overeager look of big rooms in institutions such as hospitals and churches and schools. Everything seemed fake, contrived. There was no warmth about anything in these kinds of rooms. All the ghosts of a million different meetings were hanging in here. All the same words, passed around from meeting to meeting. Same "facilitator." Same fake words. Same fake hope.

Then I looked a little harder at Mason. I didn't remember his introduction, from when we'd gone around the circle, because I hadn't really been listening that hard. Especially not after Lance Lansing's mom gave us her life story.

"So," I said, "before we do our list, can I ask you something?"

"Sure."

"Which of your family members is hurt?"

"My brother Rick."

"Oh."

I wanted to ask him for more information, but I'd already been so rude that I thought he might be rude right back.

Luckily, Mason spoke again. I didn't have to ask him anything. He just started talking about it.

"He was riding his bike and got hit by a car," he

said. "It's funny. He always wears his bike helmet. *Always*. But this one time, he didn't. He wasn't wearing it. He was just going over to a friend's house—it's, like, three minutes away—and that was the one time he wasn't wearing his helmet."

I didn't say anything, so Mason kept talking. "This guy ran a stop sign. That's how it happened. And you know what? He didn't even hit my brother all that hard. It wasn't like he was speeding or anything. But Ricky went flying over the handlebars. He landed on the sidewalk. On his head."

"How old is he?"

"He's eleven," Mason said. "I'm fourteen." A good minute or so passed. Maybe two. At least it seemed that long. Then Mason said, "How about you?"

"Thirteen."

He laughed. He had a nice laugh. "No, I meant— what happened to your family? Why are you here?"

So I wasn't the only one who hadn't been listening during the introductions. Kind of makes you wonder why they even *do* introductions at those things, because nobody ever seems to really be listening.

"It's my dad," I said. "He was wounded in Iraq. In

the war." I felt stupid for adding "in the war." I mean, why else would somebody be in Iraq? An American, I mean?

But Mason didn't laugh. He said, "So your dad's a soldier."

"No." I shook my head. "He was just sent over there with the National Guard. He's not a soldier."

Mason looked at me.

"Yeah," he said. "He's a soldier."

We only went back to family therapy night a couple of times. I think Mom decided it just wasn't worth all the aggravation of getting us there, of finding somebody to stay with Dad, and all the rest of it. And it was the pretty much the same for Mason's family. He had come with his mom and dad, but they gradually stopped coming, too.

It turns out that most families don't stick with it. They come once, or maybe twice, but then they get busy and they probably figure it's not all that helpful, anyway, to sit in a big room with a bunch of strangers and tell your sad stories. I know how it's supposed to work: it's supposed to feel good to be with people who are going through the same ordeal. People who understand.

I did find out from Mason, who found out from his parents, that I was completely wrong about that facilitator. She wasn't making fun of us. It turns out that her sister had been in a car accident a few years ago and had a traumatic brain injury. Her sister had eventually died, but first she was in a coma for five weeks. Norma knew exactly what we were all feeling. And the only thing that kept her going, she told the group, was being in a group. Just like this one.

As usual, I'd been way too judgmental. I tend to make snap decisions about people, almost always toward the negative. But I still didn't like the idea of family therapy night. For me, all that sharing made things worse. It was like hearing a dark echo rippling its way all around the room. It was like watching a row of dominoes clack and fall in that way they do, when everything has been set up just right. The dominoes fall in that ordered line, one right after another, and that's what all of our stories sounded like to me: the same story, the same shape and color of story—even if some of the details are different—hitting each other, one by one, all around the circle.

Mason and I, though, stayed friends. I don't know why, exactly. It wasn't a boyfriend-girlfriend thing. Not at all. And it wasn't because we talked about our families, about my dad or about his brother Rick, because we didn't. There wasn't much to say about that. His brother sits in a wheelchair all day long, with his head pulled down on one shoulder, and his hands curled up in his lap. He drools so badly that they just keep a towel draped across the back of the wheelchair. Every time Mason's mother goes by, she automatically picks up the towel and wipes Rick's lips and chin. And this is a kid, Mason told me in a completely even tone, with no emotion in his voice, who'd been a terrific pitcher, a kid who ran and played and who'd won the school science fair the year before his accident. Now he didn't go to school anymore. He didn't do anything.

Mason told me these things one time, and that was it. And I told him about my dad and how we built the fort and all.

My friendship with Mason wasn't based on sharing

those stories. It wouldn't be much of a friendship, I don't think, if we just sat around talking about those things. About what had happened to our families.

When we met at the mall or talked on the phone or e-mailed, we talked about Mason's artwork or about how much I liked building things. Mason was great at art. He wanted to do graphic novels. And I told him about architecture and engineering and construction. About how I liked to fit things together. To make things.

It was a different kind of friendship. I'd never had one like it before. The thing that had brought us together—the thing that had happened to his brother Rick and to my dad—was the one thing we didn't talk about. We didn't need to, I guess. Because we knew.

I didn't have to worry about Mason. He could take care of himself. I didn't have any responsibility to make him understand about anything that had happened to my family, because it had happened to his family, too. So it was easy to be around Mason. It was a relief. I felt free. I think he felt free, too, because both of us knew.

We knew.

8. PARTY

A Christmas party.

It was Jessica Weber's idea. She and Mom were talking one day in our kitchen, and Mrs. Weber said, "Hey—let's throw a Christmas party! What do you think?"

Marcy and Robbie and I were helping to make Christmas cookies to take to school. It was a Saturday in early December. Mrs. Weber had come by to help. She was at our house at least once a week, sometimes more often, to help Mom do things—clean out a room or send letters to people about Dad's medicines or just to talk.

A lot of people had come around in the first months after Dad was back. But most of them stopped coming after a while. They didn't say they weren't coming anymore. They just didn't.

Mrs. Weber, though, kept coming. It's funny: she and Mom had never been good friends before. In fact, they barely knew each other. She was just another neighbor. But it turned out that Mrs. Weber was the one who kept coming. "You never know," Mom told me, "who your real friends are going to turn out to be. You never know."

So Mrs. Weber was there with us on the Saturday we were making Christmas cookies. We always made Christmas cookies. We'd make three or four batches of all different kinds, and we'd decorate them with red and green sprinkles. Some of the cookies we took to school. Some of them to church.

Marcy was putting sugar in the mixing bowls. Robbie was supposed to be greasing the pan, but you had to watch him. Sometimes he'd start to grease other things, too, like the canisters and the silverware. He loved to rub sticks of butter on everything he saw.

Actually, it did look pretty fun, but I was too old to pretend I didn't know better.

"A party might be good," Mrs. Weber said. "What do you think, Denise?"

Mom was sitting at the kitchen table. Index cards, with recipes written on them with a purple Sharpie, were spread out in front of her as if she was playing a card game: Snicker Doodles, chocolate chip cookies, sugar cookies, peanut butter cookies, oatmeal raisin, coconut cookies, chocolate turtles, brownies with peppermint frosting.

Mrs. Weber was standing by the counter, helping Marcy measure the sugar in the little scoop to put in the bowls.

The oven was already on. You had to preheat it before you put the cookies in. So the kitchen was warm. It was warm in all kinds of ways.

We were getting ready to put the first batch of cookies in the oven when Dad showed up. He had gotten a lot better with his wheelchair and he didn't need people to push him around all the time. He'd take himself where he needed to go—in the house, I mean. He still didn't like to go out. Except for his rehab, he didn't go out at all.

So there he was, in the doorway between the living room and the kitchen. Sitting in his wheelchair.

His hair was all grown back now. In fact, it was

too long. It looked pretty greasy most of the time. It looked like Nelson Guthridge's hair, which I didn't like at all. We hadn't seen Nelson Guthridge since that day in July.

"Hi there, Ed," Mrs. Weber said.

Dad looked at her. Sometimes he didn't answer people. But they still said hello to him.

"Hi, Daddy!" Robbie said. He held up his hands, the way people do in a stickup in a cop show on TV, and he spread out wide all five fingers, to show just how much butter you can get on your hands if you really work at it.

Dad still didn't say anything, but he looked at Robbie's hands.

There was a time, months before, when Mom would have rushed right over to Dad's wheelchair to see if there was anything he needed. No matter what she was doing, no matter how busy she was, she'd go over and stroke his shoulders or rub his forehead and try to get him to talk to us, to join in. She'd do that automatically. If he came into a room, she'd go over there beside him. He was the center of things.

But she didn't do that anymore. Not automatically, anyway. If she was folding clean clothes that she'd taken out of the dryer, or putting a Band-Aid on Marcy's finger, or cutting a peanut butter sandwich in half for Robbie, or putting on makeup at the bathroom mirror, or even just sitting and reading a magazine, she'd finish what she was doing before she went over to Dad's wheelchair. She would take her time.

So that day, while we were all there in the kitchen making Christmas cookies with Mrs. Weber, and you could feel the warm air rising from the oven even before we'd put any cookies in there, and we were all laughing and talking, I saw Dad come to the kitchen doorway and for just a second I could see what he saw:

A family.

Marcy standing on tiptoes at the counter, dumping a scoop of sugar in a bright blue mixing bowl, while Mrs. Weber kept a hand on top of Marcy's hand, to guide it.

Robbie, holding out two butter-covered hands, surrounded by three flat metal cookie sheets that he'd smeared with way too much butter.

Mom, standing in front of the oven, checking the index card to make sure she had the right temperature setting.

And me, sitting at the kitchen table, getting the next index card ready so that we could make the next kind of cookie. We usually started with sugar cookies, the easiest ones to make, and then worked our way up to the hardest ones, the ones with frosting.

Just for a second, I could see what Dad was seeing: all of us together, there in the kitchen.

All of us, except for him.

He was watching. He wasn't a part of us anymore. He couldn't be.

No matter how hard any of us tried, no matter what we did or didn't do, he was sitting in a wheelchair in the kitchen doorway. He wasn't in the group anymore.

Mrs. Weber, who wasn't even related to us, was more a part of the group than Dad was. All she had to do was walk in the kitchen and pick up a measuring cup and get to work, and she was part of us.

But Dad couldn't do that. He couldn't pick up a measuring cup because he probably wouldn't know what to do with it, anyway. He was in the doorway, just watching. He'd always be just watching.

It was a moment. One moment. Dad sat there in his wheelchair in the doorway, with his fake leg and his fake arm, while the kitchen window got all steamed up with the heat from the oven, and I thought, *He's not a part of us anymore.*

It was probably something I should've realized a long time before that, but I just hadn't.

He wasn't a part of us. And he didn't want to be, not really. He could be—they'd shown him how to be, they'd taught him how to use his fake arm until it was almost as good as using a real arm, they'd taught him how to walk with his fake leg. They'd shown him at the hospital and practiced it with him over and over again at the rehab place, but he wouldn't do it.

He never even tried. Not really.

Later, a long time later, we would realize it wasn't a matter of "trying," that what looks like something you can control—like whether you join in with your family or just sit there—isn't always under your control, after all. You wouldn't expect a person with a broken arm to throw a football, would you? But because this had to do with Dad's brain, we couldn't see the broken part, and we thought he just didn't care.

Mom looked over at him, and she said, "You need something, Ed?"

He didn't say anything back. He just used his good arm to move the wheelchair backwards, back out of the doorway and into the living room or the bedroom or wherever it was that he'd come from.

And Mom turned back to the oven dial. She moved it just a little bit. "Three seventy-five," she said. "But listen, guys. Let's remember to put it back down to two-fifty for the chocolate turtles, okay? Somebody be sure to remind me."

It was later that afternoon when Mrs. Weber starting talking about a Christmas party.

"I just think," she said, "that it would be fun. For everybody."

"A party!" Robbie yelled. "I want to have a party!"

Everything sounded fun to Robbie. Sometimes I wished I could be four years old again. For a while I'd wanted to be older, so I could drive a car and have my own money, and then I wanted to be younger, so that other people would take care of me. I couldn't make up my mind. I actually think I just wanted to be any age but the age I really was.

"Well," Mom said. "Let me think about it."

"Don't think about it, Mom," Marcy said. "Do it. Don't think about it."

Mrs. Weber and Mom laughed.

"*Yes!*" Robbie yelled, way too loud, and his fist shot up in the air. He was always way too loud.

"Okay, okay," Mom said. "You guys can relax. We'll have a Christmas party. But first we've got to get these cookies done, okay, guys? So no party-planning for now. Just cookie-baking. Okeydokey?"

Robbie cheered, except that his cheers ended up as screams, like always. Fun screams, not scared screams. He used any excuse he could find to make loud noises. Marcy clapped her hands. Mrs. Weber seemed very pleased.

A few minutes later the oven timer made that *ding!* sound that meant the cookies were ready. Mom handed the pot holders to Mrs. Weber, who used them to pull out the cookie sheet.

When she leaned over and opened the oven door, out came that hot breath of air. Mrs. Weber straightened up, holding the sheet with the brown cookies out in front of her. They looked a little too brown around the edges, but nobody said anything.

Even though we knew you had to wait for the cookies to cool before you could put the sprinkles on, Marcy was already at the kitchen table, opening up the two little plastic containers: red sprinkles in one, green sprinkles in the other. She was ready. She was always prepared.

The party was on a Saturday night, four days before Christmas.

We'd baked more cookies. And Mom had whipped up her special cheese ball, the one she always made when company was coming. Nuts were stuck all over the outside of it. The cheese ball, surrounded by a spiral assortment of crackers, was put in the middle of the plate. Marcy and I liked the crackers a lot better than we liked the cheese-ball part. Mom came over twice to tell us to stop hanging around by the crackers.

Our house was full of people. It felt weird, but it was a good weird. We knew everybody, except for a couple of extra people. There was Uncle Travis and Uncle Steve and their wives. Aunt Belinda and a friend of hers. Two of my mother's cousins, Trina and Beverly. And our grandfather—Mom's father—whose name was Henry. He didn't like us to call him "Grandpa" or "Grandfather." He always wanted us to call him "Pops." Which we did. Mom's mother had died when she was just a little girl.

Mom had said that Marcy and Robbie and I could invite some friends, too, if we wanted to, but we didn't. We just wanted to help with the party.

There were people from Dad's work. We hadn't seen them in a long time. And there was Dick Christian, an old friend of Dad's from college, and his wife. She told me her name but I forgot it right away.

Jessica and Frank Weber helped Mom with the party. Frank Weber set up chairs in the living room— he'd brought over extra chairs from their house, just in case—and he changed CDs when everybody got tired of the ones that were playing. It was all Christmas music, just like you'd expect. Jessica Weber stood in the kitchen and put small sandwiches and cookies on trays, and then she'd hand the trays to me and Marcy. We carried the trays into the living room and set them on the coffee table and the end tables by the couch.

Marcy almost dropped one of her trays. That would've been embarrassing.

People didn't seem to be eating very much. The trays were staying pretty full, for a longer and longer time.

Dad sat in his wheelchair at the edge of the living room. He looked like he was half in the room and half out of it. Mom had dressed him up in a suit, which seemed strange to me. He was in a dark blue suit with a white shirt and a red tie.

The last time I'd seen Dad in that suit was right before he left for Iraq. We went to church one Sunday—we didn't go to church a lot, but Mom thought it would be a good idea that day—and now here it was again, that dark blue suit.

Between that time and this time, so much had happened to Dad. To us. It was hard to believe it could possibly be the same suit. The exact same piece of cloth. But it was.

People went over and tried to talk to Dad. They were very polite. They didn't try to shake his hand, because they thought it might be "awkward." That was the word Uncle Steve had used when he explained it to me, in a whisper.

"Hey, Eddie," Dick Christian said.

Dad was smiling. He didn't say anything.

"You're looking good," Dick Christian said. "Glad to see you back home, bud."

Dad nodded.

There were people coming up behind Dick Christian, also wanting to say hello to Dad, so Dick Christian moved away.

Pam Gurksy, a woman who'd worked with Dad at ConPow, came up to him. She touched Dad's cheek with two fingers. I thought that was strange. But then I saw tears in Dad's eyes, which made me wonder what was going on.

I was standing beside Jessica Weber, who'd come out of the kitchen. We didn't need any more trays refilled. "God Rest Ye Merry Gentlemen" was the song on the CD player. Jessica Weber saw me looking at Dad's tears, and she looked at me and said, "The thing is, Rachel, when you've got something wrong with you—or when people think there's something wrong with you—they don't touch you anymore. They're afraid to touch you. So when they *do* touch you, it's pretty overwhelming."

I didn't know how Jessica Weber knew that, but then I remembered: her limp. I'd forgotten all about it. The better we got to know her, the more she was around, the less we noticed her limp.

The song switched to "O Come, All Ye Faithful" and then "Jingle Bell Rock." A few more people were going up to Dad and saying hello and smiling. Then they'd move away.

People started to leave the party. It was way too early, but you couldn't make them stay. I could see that Mom didn't want them to go. She seemed to get kind of mad when the people in Dad's family started putting on their coats.

"For God's sake, Travis," I heard her say to Dad's brother, in a whisper that was way too loud. "You can stick around for more than twenty minutes. A lousy half an hour, maybe? It won't kill you."

Uncle Travis pulled his arm back out of the sleeve

of his heavy coat and then he put the coat back on the bed in my parents' bedroom. Robbie had stacked up all of the guests' coats on the bed.

But then, a few minutes later, I saw Travis and his wife by the front door again. Their coats were on. This time, they didn't stop to say good-bye to anybody. They just left.

Uncle Steve was arguing with some guy in the corner. The other man was wearing an old army jacket and blue jeans. He looked a little bit like Nelson Guthridge but he wasn't Nelson Guthridge.

"You gotta admit," the guy in the old army jacket was saying, "it's a war that don't make no sense. I mean, whose side are we on, anyway? What the hell does it have to do with *us*? What are we fighting for, exactly?"

"Freedom and democracy," Uncle Steve said. He always argued a lot, with a lot of different people. I'd once heard Uncle Travis say that if Uncle Steve ever worked as hard as he argued, he'd be a millionaire.

"Freedom?" said the guy in the old army jacket. "Freedom for who?"

"For us. And for the Iraqis."

"Oh, sure. *Right*." The guy in the old army jacket exhaled a fierce jet of air, almost as if he was trying to blow out a bunch of candles on a birthday cake. "Yeah, yeah, I gotcha. Freedom for the Iraqis. That's why they're all getting slaughtered."

"Well, we're not doing that," Uncle Steve said. "Those are the insurgents."

"No, buddy-boy, that's *us*," said the guy in the old army jacket. "Every day we stay over there in that hell, we're making things worse."

"That's crazy." Steve had moved closer to the guy. They were both talking louder now, loud enough to be heard over the music on the CD player. Everybody else had pretty much stopped what they were doing and were watching them.

"It's not crazy," the guy said. "Why are we there, anyway? Why are we even *over* there?"

"I told you. Freedom and democracy."

"And I'm telling *you*. It's a waste of time. Worse— it's a waste of human lives." The guy in the old army jacket held up his right thumb and jerked it toward the corner where Dad was sitting. "Just ask your brother about that whole freedom and democracy thing, will ya? Ask the guy in the wheelchair. Then get right back to me on that, okay?"

It happened so fast that nobody had a chance to do anything about it. Uncle Steve grabbed the collar of the guy's army jacket and sort of threw him sideways, like you'd yank on a car door if it was stuck.

The guy didn't really fight back. He just seemed to roll up in a ball, like a caterpillar after you poke it with a stick, and then he was on the floor, as if he didn't have any choice about it. When he rolled he knocked up against one of the end tables, and the tray with all the sandwiches and cookies on it just slid right off and landed upside down. It was a mess.

Other people were shouting now, and a woman screamed. Another woman was grabbing kids' hands and pulling us back. Dad was rocking back and forth in his wheelchair, making a funny noise.

It really wasn't as wild and exciting as it sounds, though. Nobody hit anybody. There was just Uncle Steve kind of throwing the guy in the old army jacket, and the guy rolling on the floor and knocking the tray off the end table, and a lot of screaming and ducking.

That was it. And the CD player, which didn't know any better, just kept on playing Christmas songs, one after another.

Uncle Steve called us the next day to apologize. So did the guy in the old army jacket.

Mom wasn't too mad about it. What bothered her most, I heard her telling Jessica Weber when they were cleaning up after the party, was the stain on the carpet. Somebody had stepped on one of the sandwiches, the sandwiches that spilled when the tray fell down, and the mustard had gotten "ground into" the carpet, she said.

Jessica Weber helped her scrub the spot with special carpet cleaner. Pretty soon, you couldn't tell that anything had ever happened there.

Sometimes, after he'd been back for a while, we'd watch Dad put on his fake leg. He had to put on his arm and his leg every morning, like you'd put on your pants or your shirt.

I thought he might be embarrassed to have us watch him do that, but he wasn't. He didn't seem to care whether anybody was watching him or not.

He'd get infections sometimes, around the places where his leg and his arm joined the rest of him, the real parts. Infections are very, very serious. Twice he had to go into the hospital because of the infections.

Not the army hospital. Not Walter Reed. He went into the regular hospital. Dad wasn't a soldier anymore, Mom told us. So he didn't go to the army hospital.

I didn't tell her about what Mason had said. About the fact that Dad would always be a soldier now.

Not that it was always bad. It wasn't always bad.

Sometimes, we'd have fun. There were times when Dad still liked to laugh. If you could make him laugh, then things were okay. More and more often, he was able to laugh.

Robbie was the best at making Dad laugh. Robbie would make funny faces and act goofy, which was annoying most of the time—Robbie, Mom said, never knew "when enough was enough"—but because it seemed to make Dad happy, we didn't mind Robbie so much anymore.

Robbie had taught Dad how to high-five again, with his good hand. And you'd see them do that all the time, high-fiving each other. Robbie would do something silly and then he would laugh and Dad would laugh and they'd high-five each other.

Once, Robbie tried to get Dad to high-five him with his prosthesis.

Dad wouldn't do it.

Robbie stood on the left side of Dad's wheelchair, the side with Dad's fake arm, and tried to get Dad to high-five him that way. Dad wouldn't try. He just waited for Robbie to go around to the other side.

That kind of thing would have made me mad. I probably would've gotten mad at Dad for not even trying. It would've been one of those times when my thoughts were ugly and dark, when I was ashamed of myself. But Robbie didn't care. He just went right on, like it was no big deal.

9. SKY

In the spring, Mom decided that Dad couldn't live with us anymore. Not for a while, anyway.

"It's as much for his sake as for ours," she said. She was talking to Aunt Belinda on the phone. It was a Wednesday night. Mom had already talked to me and Marcy and Robbie about it. She'd made some "arrangements," she told us. Now she had to tell Dad's family.

Marcy and I were doing our homework at the kitchen table while Mom talked on the phone. Robbie was getting ready to put on his pajamas. They were red, with little yellow-and-brown airplanes on them. Mom had just finished giving him his bath, and he liked to run around naked for a while before he put on his pajamas. We used to laugh at him when he did that, but we were so used to it now that we didn't laugh anymore. We hardly even noticed.

I don't know where Dad was right then. I lost track of him a lot these days. But there weren't a lot of places he could be. So you didn't really wonder too much about it. He was back in Mom and Dad's bedroom, I guess. Where else would he be? That's pretty much where he always was.

"It's not ideal," Mom was saying into the phone, "but for the time being, it's the right thing to do. For him and for us. I just can't see any other way." A pause. Aunt Belinda must've been arguing with her, because Mom said, in a sharp voice, "For God's sake, Belinda, I *have* thought about it. You think I haven't? You think I just woke up one morning and decided this?"

Robbie was having trouble getting his pajama top on the right way. He'd tried twice, and he kept ending up with the little tag tickling his chin.

So Mom put the phone between her shoulder and her cheek, so she could use both hands to help him while she kept on talking to Aunt Belinda.

"I know," Mom said into the phone, yanking at Robbie's pajama top. "I know, Belinda. I *know* that. Do you think I'm not fully aware of that?"

Mom's voice sounded irritated. I could tell she

didn't much like what Aunt Belinda was saying back to her.

"Fine," Mom said. "Fine. Then *you* try it, okay? *You* try living this way." A pause. "Well, I don't want to get upset either, Belinda, but you're not around here every day. Nobody is. It's just me. Me and the kids. We're the ones who have to live here. So when you try to tell us how to run our lives—"

Mom stopped. It sounded like Aunt Belinda had interrupted her. Then Mom went on, "Well, that's what it seemed like, Belinda. It seemed like you were trying to tell me what I ought to be doing. And listen, you really don't have the slightest idea, okay? Not the *slightest*. So don't you tell me—" Aunt Belinda must have interrupted her once more, because Mom stopped talking again.

Robbie's head popped up through the neck hole of his pajama top. He was grinning. Mom had gotten him all straightened out. The tag was in the back, where it belonged.

His hair was sticking up. He'd pulled the pajama top on and off so many times that it totally messed up his hair. Even though she was on the phone, Mom rubbed it to make it stick up even more, which made us all laugh. Then Mom poked Robbie in the belly. He started giggling so hard I was afraid he might choke.

Mom was talking into the receiver again. "Well, I didn't call to argue with you, Belinda. I really didn't. I called to tell you what I've decided. You and Steve and Travis and anybody else—you can do whatever you want to do. If one of you wants to try it, well then—fine. Be my guest. *Be my guest.*" There was a hardness in Mom's voice that I didn't like. But I was also kind of mad at Aunt Belinda for arguing with her like that. I knew Mom was doing the best she could. I was there every day. I knew.

And then Mom stopped the whole phone call, just like that. She didn't even say good-bye to Aunt Belinda. I'd never seen Mom do that before.

Mom pulled the phone back from her ear and she looked at it—we could hear Aunt Belinda's voice still coming out of it—and then Mom pushed the OFF button with her finger and put the phone face-first on the kitchen table. She didn't do it with a slam. She placed it there very carefully. She stared at the phone for a moment, and then she turned very quickly toward Robbie and scooped him up and stuck him on her lap. He was wiggling and squirming, which is what he always did.

"How's my Mr. Clean?" Mom said. "How's my super, super, *super* clean little boy?"

The thing is, Mom tried. I know how hard she tried. Because I was there.

You can't know about a family unless you're inside that family. Nobody can tell you what it's really like. They can tell you stories and you can look at pictures, but you don't know. Being part of a family is like being inside one of those snow globes, one of those pretty little things you turn upside down and shake back and forth to get the stuff inside to fall down like snow. You can look out and the people outside can look in, but that's all you can do. Just look. You don't know what it feels like to be on the other side.

The money we were getting wasn't enough to take good care of Dad. Somebody needed to help him with just about everything he did, and if Mom was that person, then she couldn't work full-time and she couldn't take care of us, too. Dad was supposed to be a lot further along with his rehab by now, but he just wasn't. There was no point in yelling at him. Or getting sarcastic. Sarcasm didn't do any good at all.

Life is about making choices, Mom said. That is the kind of thing adults like to say: "Life is about making choices." A simple, easy sentence. But there was nothing simple or easy about the time when Dad had a bad infection and had to go to the emergency room, and Marcy had pneumonia, and Mom had to figure out how to take care of Dad and Marcy at the same time.

Or about the night when we were ready to go to Marcy's play at school and we smelled something, and it turned out that Dad had peed on himself. We were all late to the play because Mom had to clean him up. It turns out that the brain tells you when you have to go to the bathroom. It tells you when you have to wait to go, too. And when it doesn't send you the right signal, you go anyway, and then you're in trouble.

Everything was hard. *Everything* was hard. And it

wasn't like we could talk to Dad about how hard it all was, this weird new life.

I knew it was hard for Marcy in ways that it wasn't for me. She had a lot of friends, and before Dad's injury, they'd play at our house most of the time. From the driveway, where we had this great basketball backboard that Dad had put up, you could hear the *pocka-pocka-pocka* sound of somebody dribbling, and then a lot of shouting as everybody went after the loose ball. None of Marcy's friends could dribble very well. And if they played inside, they were always chasing each other around and running into things and screaming.

After Dad was back home, things were pretty tense when Marcy's friends came over. Dad hated the noise. It got him very upset. He'd rock back and forth, making this strange whimpering sound. And so Marcy's friends finally just stopped coming around. How could you blame them? They couldn't play in whispers. They were kids. They liked to run around and yell. That's what kids do.

It was easier for me because I could leave. I could meet my friends other places. Nobody had to go with me. But Marcy and Robbie were pretty much trapped at home. Trapped with Dad.

I knew I was a little bit luckier. I guess that's a funny way to put it: "luckier." As if any of us felt lucky about anything. But I was. I could get out of the way of things for a little while. I could escape.

I saw them once. They didn't know I was watching.

I wasn't trying to snoop. It was late at night, and I couldn't sleep. That happened to me in those days. I would go to sleep, but then I would wake up again. This time was a lot like that other time in the middle of the night, the time when I'd heard my mother on the phone in the kitchen, the time when she said those things about Dad. About him not being a whole person anymore.

Only this time, Mom wasn't on the phone. She was in the living room. She was standing beside Dad's wheelchair. The lamps were all turned off, and you'd think everything would be dark, but the moon was pretty bright that night. The brightness filled the picture window, like something big and soft and endless. It made things look painted. Not with a color, but with light.

I stood in the hall, just out of sight. Do parents know how much their children see and hear in a house? Not on purpose, but just because we're always around? We move in and out of rooms and we drift through doorways and we slide into hidden spaces. We're smaller than they are, and quicker, too. We see a lot, even if we don't mean to. Even if we don't want to. We pick up stray words here and there. We know shapes and colors. We can measure things with a fast, efficient glance.

Dad was wearing the light blue bathrobe he always wore. He almost never got dressed these days. Dad's head was tilted to one side. He had his arm—his real arm—wrapped around Mom's waist. She was wearing a T-shirt and sweatpants and socks. She was looking down at Dad's head, and she had reached out with one hand and she was touching the top of his head softly, gently. She touched it with just her fingertips, the way you'd touch a baby, or a flower, or anything really fragile, anything you didn't want to take a chance on hurting. She touched the top of

Dad's head with her fingertips. Then her fingertips traveled down the side of Dad's head, over his ear, and across his cheek.

Just as Mom's hand brushed his cheek, Dad took his real arm away from Mom's waist. He put his hand on top of her hand. And then he turned his head so that her hand was on top of his mouth, and I think he kissed her hand. I think that's what he did.

"Oh, Eddie," she said. "Oh, Eddie."

It wasn't much more than a whisper. The two words moved in and out of her like a regular breath, the kind she took thousands of times a day. In and out. In and out. And steady, like ocean waves. We'd gone to the beach for summer vacation a long time ago, before Robbie was even born, and when you first see those waves, you think it has to be the same wave, reaching for the land over and over again, hoping to stay this time. But it can't. It never does. It gets dragged back. That's what Mom's words sounded like. Her voice was so soft and so low. But I think that's what I heard.

"Oh, Eddie," she said.

She kept her hand there on Dad's lips, and he

closed his eyes. Everything I saw in the living room—the couch, the chairs, the coffee table, the big window, the wheelchair, Dad's hand, the tears on Mom's face—looked sort of silvery in the moonlight. Mom and Dad were still.

They stayed like that for a long time.

Once, way before anybody I knew had ever heard of a place called Iraq, Dad took me with him to the hardware store. This was even before we'd built the fort. I'd never seen lumber like that, all stacked up in neat sheets, piles and piles of it, long rows of it, in all kinds of sizes. The smell was great. It was like being out in the woods, only better, because you didn't have to watch where you were stepping.

Dad had some other things to get, too. He needed a new valve for the toilet, and some screws, and a new bit for his drill. The bit, he told me, was an eleven-sixteenths. But then we went over to the area where they kept the wood, and that's the part I liked best. We just stood there for a minute, taking it all in. The aisle was very wide, and on each side, the piles of lumber were stacked so high that you couldn't possibly reach the top board without a ladder. Maybe not even then. It looked like all the wood in the world was gathered right there.

"Can I help you with something?"

One of the hardware-store clerks had come up behind Dad. The clerk was a high-school kid, skinny, with pimples smeared across his face and neck. He had both hands shoved hard into the back pockets of his jeans. He wore a white shirt and a bright orange vest. They made them wear bright orange vests. Nobody would've worn them on purpose.

"No thanks, Kenny," Dad said. "Just looking around."

Kenny. Dad called him Kenny. The fact that my father knew the clerk's name seemed wonderful to me. It meant Dad was a regular. It meant he was part of all this, part of the universe of cut lumber, these endless towers of wood. If you had wood and the right tools, you could do anything. Dad told me that once. He said it easily, not like he was trying to teach me some kind of lesson, but like it had just occurred to him, like he was saying it out loud at the same time he was thinking it.

I don't remember what we bought that day, except for what we came for—the valve and the screws and the drill bit. I don't know if we actually took home any lumber. But for a long time after that, I thought about those big stacks of wood heading all the way up to the ceiling, spreading out across each side of the aisle, and about how it felt to have my father's hand on the back of my neck. His hand had just stopped there naturally, while we stood there, looking up at all the wood in the world.

And so Dad went away.

First he came back home, and then he was gone again.

I would like to say that there was this huge change in our lives, that we cried all the time and that we missed him so much.

Yes, we missed him. Of course we did. But it wasn't a huge change.

Even after he came back, it wasn't like he was really there. So when he went away again, it wasn't like losing our father. I don't really know what it was like.

Okay, maybe it was like this. Have you ever thrown a rock into the ocean? Just a little stone you find on the beach maybe, something smooth and white and tiny? You throw it in, and nothing happens. The ocean is so big. You can stand there throwing in rocks all day long, you can use up every single stone you find in the sand, and it doesn't matter. The water just folds right over everything.

Sometimes, after Dad came back, that's what it seemed like: like he was a rock, and we were the ocean, and no matter what he did or didn't do, the ocean would keep on going. It would just close over the top of him. You couldn't find him anymore, out in the middle of that ocean, no matter how hard you looked. And if he called your name, you probably wouldn't be able to hear him, either.

Dad went to a place where they could take care of him. "In fact, they can take a lot better care of him than we can," Mom said. "They're professionals."

The place was about an hour's drive from where we live. There were other people there with brain injuries, too. And while some of the people had been there for years, others were new, like Dad. Some stayed for the rest of their lives. Some stayed for a while, and then they went home again.

That was the plan, Mom told us. Dad could stay there until he got better, until things settled down a little bit, and then he'd come home.

"Do you mean it?" I asked her one day, about a week after they'd moved Dad into his new home. We were alone in my bedroom. She had just hemmed up a pair of pants for me. I wanted to wear them to school the next day, so I was trying them on. The hem was perfect.

"What?"

Mom seemed startled by my question. She was sitting on the edge of my bed, while I stood in front of her, hands on my hips, in my new pants. We'd been talking about ordinary things, regular things. Not the deep and hard ones.

I said, "Do you really think he'll ever come home again?"

My mother gave me a look I'll never forget. It wasn't angry or sad. She knew I wasn't challenging her, or judging her, the way Dad's family had judged her. I was asking her to tell me the future. When you want to know the future, all you have to do is look at your parents. It's funny: everybody talks about kids being the future, but that's not how it really is. That's backwards. Your parents are the future. They are where you will be, just down the road. When you see them, you see yourself. Not just what you're going to look like. You can figure out what you'll think about the world, once you get there.

I was asking my mother to look ahead and tell me what she saw. Her answer—and I knew she'd be honest, because she was an honest person, even when you sort of didn't want her to be—would tell me how to feel about the world, my world, the one that waited for me, the one that was expecting me, with its arms open or its arms closed. I didn't know which.

So I asked her if Dad would ever come home again, and she answered quickly: "Yes, Rachel." She glanced away, then her eyes came right back to me. "I don't know," she said. "The truth is, I don't know."

And that was okay, somehow. If she'd left it at "Yes," I probably would've been suspicious. *Yes* is a small word, and an easy one. But *maybe*—well, it goes on forever. You could fit the whole world into that word. It's a big word, the biggest there is. You can live your whole life inside it.

We went to see him every weekend. The only weekends we'd miss were when somebody was sick.

We'd drive there on Saturday or Sunday, and sometimes we'd stop at the Dairy Queen on our way home and get ice cream. "To cheer us up," Mom would say.

The place where Dad lived now was a big flat brick building next to an even bigger parking lot. You went in the front door and there was a desk with two ladies sitting behind it. They wore pink smocks.

You'd tell them who you were there to see. They'd give you the room number and point in the direction you were supposed to go.

After the third or fourth time we were there, the ladies at the desk knew us. They'd just say, "Good afternoon" and not bother giving us the room number, because they knew we already knew where we were going.

We'd walk down the long hall. There were doors everywhere. Most of the doors were open, and you could see in people's rooms. You could see the beds with white bedspreads on them and the bedside tables with magazines and cloudy bottles of pills and sometimes big stuffed animals propped next to the lamps. Mainly bears.

There was a metal rail that ran along the hallway. People sat in wheelchairs in the doorways to some of the rooms. If you said hi to them, they would sometimes smile and answer you. Sometimes not. Sometimes the same person who said hi back to you one week would, the very next week, not say anything back at all.

And then we'd come to Dad's room.

He would be in his wheelchair, usually, sitting by his bed. They kept him very clean. He didn't pull his sleeve down over his fake arm anymore. He just put it on the armrest of his wheelchair, just like his real arm.

"Hi, Daddy," Robbie said. He was always the first

one in the room. He charged ahead of everybody else.

"Hi, guys," Dad said. "Hi, guys." He'd repeat the phrase when he looked at each one of us.

He was doing fine, the staff people told us. Just fine. He didn't seem sad or lonely or upset. In fact, they said, he'd made some friends. There were some other people there that he'd watch TV with.

They wished he would do more walking, the staff people said. They knew he could do it, but there was no way to force him to. When they said that, Mom would always nod, because she knew that, too.

We'd bring Dad balloons sometimes, or a picture that Robbie or Marcy made. When Marcy's basket-ball team photo was ready, Mom made sure we got a copy for Dad. She put it in a nice frame.

You could pick out Marcy in the picture right away: she was in the second row, third from the left, and she had a very serious look on her face. Like she was really concentrating. You could tell that if you sent her into the game, she would try her best. You could tell by her face that she would not let you down.

On our way home, after we'd visited Dad at the place where he lived now, we would talk about a lot of different things. About school. About Mom's job. She was working full-time now. She had to do that, she told us. But she also told us that she liked to work. She liked selling houses. And she was good at it.

I guess we ought to have been quiet on those rides home, and sad about Dad, but that wasn't what it was usually like. Usually we just talked, or Marcy and Robbie played the license-plate game. You're supposed to look for license plates from different states and you have to be the first person to call it out: "Kentucky!" or "Kansas!" or "Pennsylvania!" Whoever sees the most states wins the game. I didn't play, of course, because I had my iPod and I just wanted to sink down inside my music, but even if you're not playing, you can't help but notice the license plates of the cars that go by: Ohio. Indiana. Michigan. Florida. It's all you can do to keep yourself from yelling out the names of states when you see them.

Things happen in families. Changes. You may not like the changes, but they still happen.

Sometimes I miss him.

Sometimes I don't.

Sometimes I'm glad he doesn't live with us any-more, but I can't say that out loud, not even to Melanie, my best friend.

Actually, she's not really my best friend now. We just sort of drifted apart. There's Mason, but he doesn't go to my school. I have another friend named Beth Ann. Mason and Beth Ann didn't know me before, which is better, I think.

To tell you the truth, though, I don't like them as much as I liked Melanie. We had a lot of adven-tures when we were kids. That's not the kind of thing you just walk away from. And Melanie knew my dad before his accident. That puts her in a special category.

But things change.

These days, I think a lot about the sky in the pictures Dad sent us from Iraq.

That sky. So much whiter than the sky over here. Brighter, too.

If you look at the faces of my father and his friends in those pictures, it's almost like the light from that sky is working its way into their eyes and their skin. It's moving through them, slowly but steadily.

If you looked at those pictures again in ten years, twenty years, forty, a hundred, I'd bet you anything that the faces would be just about gone. The bodies, too. The sky would've taken over completely.

You could try to figure out where the people in those pictures had been standing, where the hard edge of each body had once been outlined against the white sky of Iraq, but you'd never know for sure. Not really.

There'd just be sky and more sky. Spreading out, arching over everything. It's kind of like a family, I guess. No matter what happens, it stretches on forever. You can't get away from it. You can't get to the end of it.

Even when you think it's not part of you anymore, even when you think you've left it far behind, you look up.

And there it is. There it is.

A NOTE TO THE READER

The number of U. S. casualties in the wars in Iraq and Afghanistan is low, compared to previous wars. But according to recent reports, 10 to 20 percent of all soldiers returning from those conflicts show symptoms of traumatic brain injury. Most of these injuries are concussions of mild to moderate severity. Yet several thousand veterans have returned with a brain injury as severe as that endured by Rachel's father.

Explosive devices such as roadside bombs — common in Iraq and Afghanistan — are a frequent source of brain injuries. That is why brain injury is routinely referred to as the "signature injury" of these wars. The reason for the high number of survivors with brain injuries comes, ironically, from a positive development: medical advances mean that many more soldiers with severe injuries now are saved. But that means they will struggle with brain injuries—injuries from which, in previous wars, they would have died—for the rest of their lives. And so, of course, will those who love them.

As a writer for the *Chicago Tribune*, I was the author of a three-part series about traumatic brain injury. Each year, according to the Brain Injury Association of America, more than a million and a half Americans are diagnosed with traumatic brain injury. Many more may go undiagnosed. For the series, I followed five people as they underwent rehabilitation for severe brain injury. I spent time with their families, as well.

Later, as I read about American soldiers returning from Iraq and Afghanistan with brain injuries, a story began to unfold in my mind. It was a story about an ordinary family forced to deal with an extraordinary loss.

This book is about one young girl's journey. It is a journey undertaken thousands of times each year by children, and other family members, of people with brain injuries.

ACKNOWLEDGMENTS

My dear friend Marja Mills read the initial chapters of this story and insisted that I finish. I would sometimes grow discouraged; she never did. My gratitude to her is beyond measure.

Elizabeth Law at Egmont USA is a brilliant editor, possessed of a keen eye and a generous heart. Many thanks to her, as well as to her colleagues Nico Medina and Mary Albi; my agent, Stuart Krichevsky; my niece, Julianna Poole, another early reader of these pages; and Susan Phillips.

My love of literature for younger readers was reawakened by Ann Marie Lipinski, former editor of the *Chicago Tribune*, and my *Tribune* colleague Elizabeth Taylor.

Several years ago, the staff and patients at the

ACKNOWLEDGMENTS

Rehabilitation Institute of Chicago trusted me to tell their stories. What I learned there became a crucial part of what you read here: the quiet daily heroism of those who struggle with brain injuries.